OSKAR

and

NINETEEN OTHER
UNEXPECTED TALES

—by—

DAVID C. SHELLEY JONES

First published 2025 by David C. Shelley Jones

Produced by Independent Ink
independentink.com.au

Cover design by Catucci Design
Edited by Jane Smith
Internal design by Independent Ink
Typeset in Adobe Caslon Pro by Post Pre-press Group, Brisbane
Cover images: Eugenegg/istockphoto.com, stsmh/istockphoto.com

ISBN 978-1-7640682-0-8 (paperback)
ISBN 978-1-7640682-1-5 (epub)
ISBN 978-1-7640682-2-2 (kindle)

CONTENTS

THE
TANK
—

BEFORE THE FIRE HARRY AND BERYL WERE TALKING ABOUT ED. Ed was the best man at their wedding forty-one years earlier. They lost touch with Ed many years ago. Beryl tried to send a card last Christmas, only to have it returned, "address unknown".

Do you think he's still alive, Beryl, love? Harry asked.

Well, he was only a few years older than us, so maybe.

And wasn't there a cancer operation? When was that, a decade ago? Remember the letter from Sheila? Last we've heard.

So maybe yes and maybe no.

He was a good bloke.

*

After the fire the steers come back to lick water from the leaking tank. The tank is next to a burned-down shed. The shed is not far from a burned-down house, now nothing much more than a chimney and foundation stones. Water trickles away from the tank in small rivulets that snake through the blackened grass, down towards the track, towards the main road. The main road is a long way away. It is a big block in the west of New South Wales.

Harry remarks that the steers are back, but Beryl says nothing. She's been getting quieter, and Harry's worried. Sometimes her goose-bumped body drifts up against his and he can feel her cold, shrivelled flesh. Harry thinks he has a better chance than Beryl, although they're probably both stuffed. Beryl is as thin as a whip. Harry was thin too once, when he was an accountant. Now he is all farm-work muscle and beer blubber.

They have been treading water for, he guesses, seven hours. The fire front came suddenly with a change of wind. About mid-morning.

He looks up at the small circle of sky and sees that it is turning a deeper shade of blue. Then he works his legs hard for a moment so that he can press both palms flat against the corrugated iron and feel the heat outside. He knows that if the water hasn't warmed up by now, it won't.

Sometimes, as much as for something to do as to give his arms a rest, Harry draws in a big breath and relaxes his muscles and lets himself sink until his toes sift into the slimy bottom of the tank. Into the God-knows-what. He has already felt animal bones in one spot – taking note to fix the mesh on the gutters if they ever get out. He and Beryl were as sick as dogs a few months ago. Might be the explanation.

When he returns to the surface his arms resume describing neat circles on the flat summit of collected rainwater.

*

Harry and Beryl have discovered a method of getting the odd break, although it's almost more trouble than it's worth. The tank has an indentation, a ding from the rear tray of Harry's ute when it was laden with fence posts. It is possible to get a partial foothold, right or left depending on the direction faced, but then the opposite arm has to work harder to maintain balance. They use this now and then, and they also try different styles of treading water. These generally involve uniform arm movements with legs moving about randomly like separate disconnected things. They already can barely feel their legs and eventually their limbs will fail and they will sink and that will be that. They had not counted on the height of the tank and the depth of the water. They had not thought about the smoothness of well-tooled iron.

Were they to see that the ding in the tank was leaking, they might be happy, although the tension would have been unbearable. The size of the drops, the rate of the drops, the volume of the tank. The maths would have been too hard. Even for a former accountant.

*

They will come. They will find us, Harry says.

Yes, someone. Rhonda, maybe. Mrs Heron. Yes, Mrs Heron will notice we haven't been in today.

Yeah. Damn right. You're right, says Harry.

And they return to silence. They have been over the scenarios dozens of times, but no-one comes, and the hours pass, and they grow colder and weaker.

After a while, Rob comes up again.

What if he hears about what's happened and stops and tries to call? says Beryl.

Not bloody likely, says Harry. He won't be giving us another thought. Would have been nice if he'd stayed with us. Had Christmas with his own family. He's only been seeing her for five months, for God's sake.

So it's down to Rhonda and Mrs Heron, they agree.

*

And as they talk, Rhonda's busy feeding her children on the veranda of the house next door. On the next twenty-acre block. Behind the stand of snow gums.

And Mrs Heron is standing on the pavement of the high street while the sliding glass doors of her store open and close behind her.

And Rob, who borrowed the car at daybreak, is heading north with a head full of Red Bull and the music blaring, thinking of his girlfriend with the great figure and the lovely smile.

*

Rhonda's children sit in highchairs, and Rhonda sits facing them in an old bentwood chair she found when they moved in. They are out on the back veranda because it is too hot inside the house. The tin roof creaks, slowly cooling and contracting, as the sun settles behind the hills. Late afternoon light filters through the charcoal skeletons of trees to reach the backyard where a tricycle lies on its side, the plastic seat dripping over the frame like a melted, re-set party cake. Everything is ash. In the distance a lame kangaroo, half its hide tanned and blackened, forages along the ring-lock fence.

*

Beryl gets another cramp, and Harry nearly drowns himself massaging her calf until it passes.

*

Rhonda's children are perhaps eighteen months and three years old. It's hard to tell. Wrists, elbows, knees, eyes are all nearly lost in rolls of baby fat. The smallest, Cheyenne, turns her head away to resist another spoonful of custard. She is cranky, as her fat little baby legs barely fit through the leg-holes and her thighs are chafing.

Please, Cheyenne, Mummy loves you so much. Please eat for Mummy.

No, no, no, says Cheyenne. She purses her lips tightly and turns her head away. There are pools of rejected dinner at the base of the highchair. Spilled vanilla custard seeps down between the jarrah planks to the dark, damp earth below, to the world of the black cat. Rhonda has never seen the cat, but the corpses of little rodents on the doorstep attest to its existence. She assumes Schrödinger left the cat behind when he sold the house next door and moved on. Schrödinger had a lot of cats. It was one his quirks.

*

Trust that German bloke to have built such a bloody big tank, says Harry.

They had bought the house from Schrödinger. Schrödinger was a poor German immigrant made good. He had built the house himself, a robust house of solid German foundations. Unfortunately, the rest was made of wood and the house was, therefore, ultimately doomed.

Schrödinger had told them that he would have liked to have built the house out of stone and mortar, in the German style, but he hadn't been able to find enough stone.

*

It is Christmas Eve and one hour from closing time. Mrs Heron looks down the gently sloping high street towards the burned-out farms, towards Harry and Beryl's place. Here and there, plumes of smoke continue to puff out the memory of trees. In the foreground, everything is busy. Four-wheel drives come and go. People come and go. The atmosphere is almost jolly.

*

Early on, Harry and Beryl kept their spirits up with songs and recollections. Now they spend their time trying to tease out the fractured, intermittent outside sounds from the echoes within. Their words, their breathing, even the lapping of water: everything drops pitch and lingers, circling them in the shadows. They feel they are swimming with ghosts.

And Beryl says, sometimes I hear voices that aren't ours.

Beryl has the cat's eyes. Quite unlike Harry, who is locked in the real world a bit too much for his own good, in her opinion. A bit of spirituality, a bit of navel-gazing, never hurt anyone. Beryl's mother was a clairvoyant and lived to be a hundred. Goes to show.

Occasionally there is the hum of a car on the road beyond the track or the distant laugh of kookaburras. Recently, the creaking of the Hills hoist announced the arrival of the westerly. And so there should be wind chimes; the wind chimes on the back veranda should be ringing, deep and rich as church bells. But from the wind chimes, nothing. The house was not yet gone when Harry and Beryl climbed up and jumped in the tank. There was hope then. There is hope.

*

Mrs Heron is short and round and sixty-two years old but looks fifty. She says this is the one benefit of a plump face. She will tell anyone who listens that she doesn't like managing the supermarket, although the job suits her social inclinations. She sees herself as a student of the human condition.

She is not thinking about Harry and Beryl as she stands out on the pavement. About them not coming in to shop, even though it's Friday and their shopping day. She is thinking about Rhonda, the town anorexic who comes in several times a week. Rhonda with the bad teeth, the batik shirts and tattoos, whose partner left her soon after the birth of their first child. Went off to do some contracting work in Western Australia. Found a woman. Never returned. The usual story.

*

Sometimes Beryl stands on Harry's shoulders while Harry holds his breath with feet planted squarely on the bottom of the tank. On one occasion, Beryl managed to hook her fingers on the sharp, cruel rim of the tank, but her hands were not strong enough and she fell back into the water. She sobbed for a minute or two before pulling herself together. That's what you do. That's how you survive.

*

Rhonda puts the kids to bed and sits on the veranda having a smoke. Maybe, later, she'll think about dinner, but she's not hungry. She's never hungry. Rhonda looks out over the backyard to the black paddocks. The burned roo is nowhere in sight. There are galahs in the ruined veggie garden, though, adding little splashes of pink and grey like strange flowers suddenly in bloom. And on the veranda railing perches a line of brilliant red-and-green rosellas hoping for a feed. But Rhonda's not in the mood. She thinks about her man over in W.A. She hasn't heard from him in over nine months. Child endowments are overdue. It isn't the money, though. Does he ever think of her? Does he have regrets?

While she's lighting up a second cigarette, Rhonda remembers Harry and Beryl. She hasn't seen them since the fire, and their car is gone. They must be with relatives, she thinks. Then she wonders whether she should go over and have another look at the world of Harry and Beryl – reduced to nothing but a chimney and foundation stones and a water tank. But should she have another look?

In any event, Rhonda is tired, and she decides to get an early night. She takes a few prescription pills and regards the swing chair in the corner of the veranda where she used to sit with her man in the long evenings, making plans. Now it's laden with her attempts at pottery. The pieces are improving, she thinks. She'll use ash in the glazing next time. She's heard it can produce a nice effect. Something good will come from the fire, after all.

*

It is almost dark when Harry notices that the water level is dropping. It's obviously going to be a close-run thing.

There's a chance, love, he says to Beryl, there's a bloody chance. Hang in there, B.

And Beryl doesn't say anything at first.

Then, after a while, she says the sweetest thing.

I love you, Harry. I'd do it all again.

*

Just as Harry is commenting on the water level, Ed is taking his morning walk on an English heath. It promises to be a fine day. There is a light mist and a hint of blue sky. His dog, Graham, trots along beside him. Ed has taken to long walks since his wife died and the children moved out. While Graham is having a leak on the hedgerow, Ed's mind drifts to Harry and Beryl. Harry and Beryl. He wonders. Are they alive? Do they exist? I must drop them a line.

SIX FOOT TRACK

THE TRACK CUTS THROUGH STUNTED TREES ON WORN-DOWN mountains, very old mountains of uncertain memory. They made it six feet wide so that packhorses could pass. Untended, the track has narrowed, so that now it's barely a track at all – sufficient, though, for a man and a dog. The dog tags along behind. He knows the dog is there, but when he turns around, there is nothing, only a hint of dog – a rustle in the undergrowth, a canine smell. Sometimes, to catch it out, he turns about abruptly – but always with the same result: no dog, just an impression of dog.

When he reaches a small stream, he stops and scoops the tannin water with a green enamel mug. The mug is a reminder of his scouting days. He was a bad scout. Unreliable, untidy, profane.

He drinks and splashes water on his face, knowing that this is the easy bit, that the plateau will soon give way to ragged, sandstone cliffs, and he will be descending in a slipstream of crumbling rock. On unsure footing. Grabbing on to anything he can.

And the water in the stream will come undone, fall into the valley – a central, disorderly cascade – a halo of fine strands floating in the updraft. Like lover's hair. Like Cynthia's hair. He used to love the way she'd swing her hair loose on getting home, in their bedroom late at night, after a concert – back in the years of wonder when the band, his band, could do no wrong.

He sits for a while beside the stream, studying the fragments of sky that hang between eucalypts. He looks down at his boots, caked in mud. He looks to a far-off escarpment glowing yellow in the morning light. He cannot see the valley. It is country without middle distance.

He gets up and swings his pack to his shoulders and shouts *cooooeeee* and then stands still to listen. And all he hears is the hum of wind winding its way through the fractured landscape.

"Silly bastard. Silly bastard," he mumbles to himself and presses onwards.

He's decided they've gone on ahead. Maybe they'll be thinking he's left without them. He knows they won't be happy. The fat banker will be saying he's a loser. Kelly will be discouraging them from hanging about because she has a boyfriend waiting at the other end. And the lovely guide? She'll be worried. It's obvious she's new from the way she reads from prepared notes, boring things like how banksia need fire to germinate and how everything was once completely underwater. He's sorry to be getting her into trouble.

When he's moving, he keeps his eyes squarely on the ground ahead. Because it can suddenly become wide-angle. Precipices appear without warning. It's possible to simply walk out into space. Into the blue.

He recalls the story of a German tourist who left his hotel for a bit of fresh air and a smoke. Who wasn't seen again until they found his body years later, on a ledge, close to the top of a nearby cliff. The surprising thing was that only one leg was broken.

Apparently, everyone spent too much time searching the bottom of the valley. Which goes to show that pessimism rules.

He is haunted by the image of a rescue chopper and a stretchered, spinning man inching upwards to its jaws. "Not me," he says aloud, but he is uneasy; the red-checked shirt, the pants, the hair – a little hair has escaped the medivac shroud and blows about in the rotor wash. He imagines the man's face and sees his own: a grim rictus, an aquiline nose, full, rosy-red lips, an unshaved chin, rather square.

"Jesus Christ, not me!" he says a second time, pushing the image of the corpse out of his mind, trying to distract himself with thoughts of Cynthia. They should have worked it all out, stayed together, made babies; he should have cleaned up his act, gone to rehab. She was beautiful, perfect, brilliant and now even a little bit famous. He was an idiot.

He walks on – in his red-checked shirt and baggy shorts and boots that should have been road-tested before the hike.

He is already talking to himself and he's only been lost for two hours, which he thinks is reason to keep the pouch of dope safely tucked away. It's half empty, in any case. Some of it was smoked the night before while the guide read a book in her tent. He'd offered it around. Most of them had taken polite little drags – with the exception of Suresh. He had the tip of his joint glowing like a furnace, and he'd had to snatch it back. They'd all talked and laughed until, one by one, they retired. By midnight, only Kelly remained. They'd gone on to discuss cool things like the colour of mirrors and how long it would take to listen to every song on iTunes. He'd made a pass. She wasn't interested.

*

And now here he is, lost, looking like a total fool. Which, he has to admit, he is.

*

The next twenty-four hours are a blur, just puffs of memory passing like clouds. The emergence from bush. The brightness of sky curving over and around and down to the roof of trees far below. The valley waiting. He had once been told that wilderness is always waiting. By whom? He cannot remember.

There is a path on the valley floor that is barely a path, and he moves along it like a shadow, unused to the silence of soft ground, in a graveyard of fallen trees, with giant ferns blooming in the half-light, roots branching and sifting in the thick, black, worm-racked soil, flashing at him like pieces of bone.

This is the land before Adam and Eve, he says to himself, before dinosaurs even.

Occasionally, somewhere in the canopy, up in the dry, clear, thin white air, a whipbird whistles a long, drawn-out, middle C. Finding comfort in this sound, he responds by calling *cooooeee* again and again and again. Until he is hoarse.

Then he walks on, making arbitrary decisions on paths that fork and fork again, on looping paths that return to the beginning. On false passages. In a world without reference to anything. Not to time. Not to place. No sun by day. No stars by night. He can't remember much about stars in any case, except that the Southern Cross is southern.

*

Lunch on the first day was a Mars bar at the base of a boulder with an overhang.

Afternoon tea was a joint while sitting on a log at yet another fork in the track.

When the light grows thinner, he soothes himself by making plans, deciding that the evening meal will comprise a Mars bar and a second joint. But he's soaked his matches. Late in the afternoon, at the base of a cliff, perhaps not far from where he started, he had heard the sound of falling water, like a distant rain shower. As he approached, the trees parted and he could see water tumbling down from a dizzy patch of blue – in a perfect, even sheet. To strike a shelf of furrowed rock and make a fog of spray. To gather itself up and flow away. A neat little stream in a forest of shadows.

He found her there, veiled by falling water, Cynthia, naked and beckoning. He did his best to read her lips. Come to me, she seemed to say, come to me. Naturally, he'd marched straight in, without a moment's hesitation, and lost his footing on rounded rocks. In freezing, knee-deep water. After righting himself, he'd got up and looked around and she was gone and there was nothing for it but to proceed onwards, wet and shivering, with the dog trailing.

The night, moonless black and fearfully cold, stops him in his tracks and he slides down against a tree into a soft depression of fallen leaves. Using a torch, he selects the driest of his matches and strikes the box – but it breaks in two. He tries again with half a match and manages to make a little flame that quickly splutters out. "Please, Jesus," he says, before he tries a new match. This time a bright flame illuminates his cupping hands and he finds himself in a cave of light like in a Flemish masterpiece, or in outer space, and he lights a joint. Feeling better, he reflects on his situation – noting that there is one serviceable match left. This match is going to be the fire match.

"They're sure as shit going to buy my music after I'm gone. I didn't give up the piano for nothing. All that practice for nothing!"

His teacher had cried when he broke the news to her, that he was giving up classical music and joining a band. She told him that she could take him to the very top. He will never forget it: the mole on her neck, the faint, downy hair on her chin, the tears rolling down her powdered cheeks.

Then he gets higher and feels great and he starts to think about the good things. Cynthia. The girls. The parties. His family. Cynthia. It always comes back to Cynthia. He smiles and shivers.

The joint becomes so short that he has to hold it in a delicate pincer grip between index finger and thumb, like a crab. That is the great thing about dope, he thinks: the metaphors come thick and fast, the guitar riffs drop out of heaven. Of course, there is always the problem that inspiration in such circumstances comes in code. The punter has to be high to decipher it, so it isn't commercial. He recalls someone saying (and he wishes he could recall who all these someones were) that if you drink enough absinthe, it becomes clear that van Gogh painted in straight lines. But you've got to drink lots of absinthe and not many people do. No wonder van Gogh died a pauper.

He considers the options while he smokes: let the joint go out, light another joint, start a fire. He lights another joint. And when it is nearly finished, he madly scratches about for leaves and twigs and attempts to start a fire with the still glowing tip, puffing at embers for all he is worth, failing and swearing. He tries to light a third match without result.

*

They came for him that night. They must have been waiting. The spirits floated in like unmoored boats, some familiar, some vaguely recognised, some unknown.

First came the spirit guide, floating in-between the ferns, gliding under the canopy of trees.

Then came Jeremy, the band's first drummer, wanting his thirty dollars back.

"You don't need thirty bucks, mate, you're dead," he said. And Jeremy told him that there was a girl over at the bar and that he wanted to go down to the ferry wharf with her and a bottle of Jim Beam. Jeremy was always hard to refuse.

"So, there are girls in heaven?"

"Who said anything about heaven, I don't know where the fuck I am."

"I'm sorry about letting you go, Jeremy."

"That's okay, man. I can see the big picture now. I was too unreliable, wasn't I?"

"Yes, you were, Jeremy."

"Was I any good, though? That's what I want to know."

"You were pretty good. You could have been better."

"The booze, the pills?"

"Yeah."

"Did you love me, though? Did you all love me?"

"We loved you, Jeremy. We felt terrible. You shouldn't have done it, mate."

"I wouldn't do it now."

"Jesus Christ, Jeremy, it's a bit late to say that!"

"I know."

"If we could do it all again, we would have looked after you better. We were selfish arseholes back then."

"It is what it is."

"Yeah, it is what it is."

And he fell asleep again and the cold crept up, its icy roots permeating every layer of clothing, burrowing inward towards his warmly beating heart.

Mrs Granger, the headmistress, with her hearing aid and Eau de Cologne, came next. "You've got to get your act together, my boy, before it's too late. You could do great things, you know."

And then came Cynthia.

"We nearly had it all," he said to her.

"We did have it all, baby," she replied.

"Don't tell me you're dead."

"I'm not dead, baby, I've just come to mess with your head. 'Cause you deserve it; you're a selfish bastard. You take more than you give."

And, before he had a chance to apologise to Cynthia, she was gone.

And there were others.

Just before daybreak, there was a young man he didn't recognise. The young man asked him: "Do you remember December?"

He could not.

*

Sometime during the night, a tree fell. It must have been a very big tree. It shook the ground and woke him up. He later remembered thinking: *I am here for the tree, man, I'm here, that's what it's all about, being here. Here not there.*

*

He wakes to the laugh of a kookaburra in the pale, grey light of dawn and sets off, hungry and light-headed, to what he hopes is the western side of the valley, measuring time with dry-mouthed, whispered songs, navigating by the length of shadows. The dog follows, hanging off like a mangy mongrel. He comes upon further crossroads, as he knew he would.

The track ahead forks three ways and he hasn't the faintest idea which to choose. Despondent, he stops walking, convinced he is no longer a lucky man, and sits on a log, filling in the time inspecting his remaining matches, dropping them one by one into his upturned cap. When he finds an almost-dry match, he lights up and has a smoke while the day grows brighter. Then Jesus comes along, white-robed and bearded, walking towards him with gentle, even steps. He has a wooden walking stick. He has kind eyes. He even has stigmata. There are needle tracks on his wrists.

"Mate, am I glad to see you," he says as he gets up, unconsciously tucking in his shirt, taking off his cap, smoothing down his hair, aware that "mate" is too familiar a term for Jesus. If it really is Him.

He suggests a round of Texas hold 'em poker to break the ice, knowing that Jesus is sure to win – although Jesus probably doesn't have any money either, there being no shops in the wilderness. But Jesus declines and walks on down the track, gesturing to one of the three paths, before disappearing into the eternal gloaming of rainforest. Without even giving him the opportunity for a selfie.

He takes the path chosen by Jesus and emerges late in the day, in the car park of Jenolan Caves, half-running, half-rolling down a steep embankment until coming to a stop on bitumen between a tour bus and a campervan.

*

The rest was disappointing. No squark of two-way radios. No relieved search and rescue personnel. There was nothing for it but to cadge a lift to town. Where there was no office. Where there was no hiking company. Where no-one knew his guide. He went to the car park behind the supermarket, to the space next to the stacked trolleys, and found it empty. The car wasn't worth much, in any case. The gears were shot. The wipers didn't work.

He found half a hamburger on a bus seat and shared it with the dog. He remained there until nightfall. Not a problem to anyone. Merely a derelict in a dirty red-checked shirt asking himself if this is what it's like to be dead.

*

In the great chamber of Jenolan Caves, amidst stalactites and stalagmites, the fog of breath lifts upwards in the frigid air. Whispered words are rippling, sliding along the limestone walls. It's night and winter and very cold. Like when he was lost. All those years ago. How many years? – he doesn't know. Wandering souls lose track of time. Mountains have no memory.

Before him, his darling acolytes wait in eager anticipation. He is remarkably serene, given the circumstances, a moment that may never come again. Or maybe it will. Depending on unknown variables. But who cares? Who gives a shit? The dog has a juicy bone, and he is as ready as he will ever be: gym-toned ready, with hair grown long, the greying bits dyed black. Practised, polished to the nth degree.

He nods. The lights go off. The darkness is now total. Not even a phosphor smudge. Not even a retinal memory of light. Silence broken only by steady drops dripping down crystal cones, hanging for a bit, finding release, falling into muddy little pools on the limestone floor. Counting out the aeons. Keeping perfect time. Always. Unlike Jeremy.

Then someone coughs. The lights come on again. With startling effect. To stun dilated pupils. To razzle dazzle. And he is on the stage before them, the gathered, privileged few. With his organ, giant and rare, sitting sideways so that everyone can see. On a dais, hammered together three days earlier – each hammer blow a shock of sound.

He turns to smile. The audience is small. It had been a battle to get Parks and Wildlife to agree to anything at all. Humidity, they said. Humidity ruins the crystals. So only a small audience and a livestream to the world. Unavoidably, the ticket prices are high, very high, a million dollars a seat including champagne.

A humidity extractor hums, vermiculates, hovers like a giant silver worm above their heads. So that programs flutter upwards in rare flight.

A tuxedoed emcee says: "Silence please."

And he lives on in this before – before his fingers fly on ivory keys, before his feet dance, before the pipes sing.

SPINNING BACHARACH

"HOW MANY COUNTRY AND WESTERN SINGERS DOES IT TAKE TO change a light bulb?" someone asked recently; he can't quite remember who. He was drinking at The Lamb with some Aussie expats who were in London for a couple of days, on a break from constructing something in the Gulf. The answer was "Thirteen: one to change it and twelve to sing about how great the old bulb was." This just about sums it up: the grandeur of the unremembered past.

The joke comes to mind while he is considering the LPs on the bookcase, the real-deal type, made in the sixties and seventies when life, presumably, was great. He is pulling individual LPs out of the pile, sometimes pausing to enjoy the artwork, which can be very good or very naff. Eventually, he finds what he is looking for, and he unsleeves a disc from quite a cheesy cover and places it gingerly onto the turntable on the shelf above. With a quick puff he blows away a tiny ball of dust that is clinging to the diamond needle of the player. It blows away so easily. It blows away like vanished days.

He presses play. The needle lifts and swings out across a sea of spinning black, settling on an outer vinyl groove. Music begins – old time music, soothing music. It's Burt Bacharach. His parents always loved Burt Bacharach. This he remembers, but many childhood memories seem to be missing. Right now there are two certainties: his parents loved Bacharach, his parents loved him. There was never any deficit of love, so it's hard to imagine how things went so wrong.

Until the day before yesterday he hadn't seen his parents in three years; now he's seeing them twice in three days. The first time was when he picked them up from Heathrow at the ungodly hour of six and then spent the day with them visiting famous London sights. The idea was to keep them going, get their clocks right. By 5 pm, they were fading and he had taken them back to a small hotel in Chelsea.

When he was helping them get their suitcases from the taxi to the hotel foyer, he apologised again for not having them stay in his flat. "I thought of putting you both on the sofa bed, but you wouldn't get a wink of sleep."

There was also an apology for the dinner party that he's planned for two nights hence. "I didn't want to throw you in the deep end so soon, Mum and Dad, but Henry and Florence are leaving for Africa on Friday, and I really want you to meet my friends. They've been so good to me. They've made all the difference."

He left Australia on bad terms with his parents, but now he wants to make amends. He was pleased to see they felt the same, that it was time to move on. Nothing was actually said along these lines; it was understood.

*

On the night of the dinner party, wind is whipping down from the North Sea. News footage shows it stripping leaves from autumn trees. The roots of ancient oaks are lying sideways on bridle paths. In Maidstone, a power line is down.

Everyone has been told to come at seven, and it's seven-thirty and his parents are not there. Just when he is on the verge of allowing himself to worry, the doorbell rings. In moments the two most important people in his life are right before him, brimming with parental affection. Things are coming back to normal. Their old Damian is back.

"Took the Tube in the wrong direction," says Damian's mother, "Your father was certain we were going the right way."

"You were the one who raced to get on it, Lorraine; you didn't give me a chance to check."

"Anyway, here we are, darling," says his mother, giving him a kiss. "And what a lovely flat you have, and in Kensington too, very flash."

"Only just in Kensington, almost Notting Hill."

"Well, we're pleased to see you doing so well, champ," says his father. His father used to call him champ when he'd done well at something.

He takes his parents into the sitting room and introduces everyone. They have to skirt around the piano, a Yamaha he cannot really play, that he bought for a song over a year ago. He has a mind to take lessons, only things keep coming up.

*

His parents are awkward at first. Inviting five contemporaries was probably unwise – too much, too soon. To make matters worse, his parents are overdressed despite him telling them exactly what to wear. What's the point of bringing nice clothes to London if you don't wear them, they said. England has always retained a sort of mythical status in the Crowley family imagination, especially his mother's; England has always been a place of dreams and aspirations, far removed from the struggle of managing five thousand acres of barely arable land. Damian's maternal great-great-grandfather had come to Australia from Devon at the end of the nineteenth century, the youngest son of moderately prosperous landholders. Youngest sons went to the colonies to make their fortune if there wasn't enough estate to go around. Daughters got dowries or a modest income from a trust. This was the way of things.

Once everyone has a drink in their hand, Damian retreats to his small kitchen to add the final touches to the meal. While working out of sight, he listens to the conversation taking place across a pair of mirrored sofas.

"Well, what do you all do?" asks Damian's father. His father will be primarily interested in whether any of them are settled down with children. Legacy is his father's obsession. Damian is an only child.

The question is efficiently answered, as he expects. The words *photographer, lawyer, art restoration, actor* and *land management* come in quick succession.

Land management is Henry.

"Oh, don't be so modest, Henry," says Alice. "Henry has a big estate in in Gloucestershire, don't you Henry?"

"Damian's a great shot you know, Mr and Mrs Crowley," says Henry. "Your son is a natural."

"Jack and Lorraine, please," says Lorraine.

"Well, Jack and Lorraine, he can bag more birds than anyone."

The subject suits Damian's father. There is talk of shooting pheasants and roos, while Damian shuffles back and forth with uncorked wine and Flemish beer in steins.

*

"This meal is amazing. I mean, I had no idea that you were into food, Damian. Really, your son is a man of many talents," says Alice, giving Damian's parents a very charming smile. Damian notes that her smiles range from wry-sardonic minimalism to a spectacular show of perfect teeth. She is lovely. She has a light brown bob, although, when he looks closely, he can see many shades of red and brown.

Responding to yet another affirmation of her son's unknown talents, Damian's mother declares that her son has "such wonderful friends", the sweet tone of her voice at odds with her interrogating eyes. What she really wants to know is this: what is going on? What is keeping her son on the other side of the world? A year was long enough. It's unlike him to be tempted by opportunity; inertia's more his style.

The flat was leased semi-furnished. It's not a big flat and it's up three flights of stairs, so the terms were very good. He was worried about the crowded seating around the dining table, but this is not proving to be a problem; in fact, the rubbing of elbows is contributing to the joviality. He had warned everyone in advance that it might be a strained evening: "They're farmers, you know, almost in the outback, and they'll be a bit jet-lagged, poor dears, so they might be overwhelmed." He had forgotten how gregarious his parents can be once they are settled in with a few drinks and convivial company. Look at them, he thinks, laughing and joking – much better company than anyone would guess.

Henry and Flo's trip is not the real reason for holding the dinner party so early in his parent's visit. The real reason is that he has to do a run to Amsterdam in a couple of days and the lease of the flat runs out in a week.

*

"How do you do the asparagus, Damian? There's something – a certain something – there; I can't work it out. It's superb."

This is Farouk, a handsome man with a thick mane of dark hair. He carries an air of self-assurance that might come from wealth. His accent is mid-Atlantic. His cuff-linked shirt and fancy watch speak of money. Possibly, he is of Egyptian or Persian origin. Damian can see his mother itching to ask him about his background, only she's too well-mannered; she's aware that unless she uses precisely the correct phraseology, she might cause offence – if not to the man himself, then to someone else at the table; and she's probably right, that's the way it is now, you have to be so careful.

"The recipe is a secret, I'm afraid, taught to me by a Michelin-starred chef. We shared a chalet in St Antons. He did a bit of cooking in the evenings – best food I've ever had, and he wasn't even trying."

The meal they are eating has been bought from a fancy take-away store on Ken. High, with a few fresh touches added. No need to point this out.

"How do you all know each other?" asks Damian's mother. Usually, his mother does most of the talking. It is unusual that tonight his father is leading the way. His father is pleased to be back in London, he says, after so many years. His father is a ball of enthusiasm. The mood suits his big frame, his ruddy farmer's face. Damian has always thought of his father as one big barrel of farmer flesh, meaning *hard* muscle, not the over-refined, fancy city-gym type muscle; his father has – had – the sort of muscle that gets things done. He's seen his father lift a seventy-kilo ram over a stockyard fence without much effort. Only, right now, Damian can't help noticing that his father's pants are hanging loosely around his waist. This never used to be the case.

His father would spend all his travel time in London if he could. It's the history, he says, a break from the eternity of bush. His mother prefers the English countryside, the soft light, the gentle scenery. His mother is petite. His mother is dynamic. She's president of the local garden society, she's on the board of the primary school.

"How does everyone know each other, then?" she asks again. It's a good question. Every face turns towards Damian. There is the hint of a smile here and there.

"Oh, I don't know," he says. "Some of us have friends in common, some of us met around the traps – parties, weekends away, that sort of thing. Alice and Theo might tell you about the few days we've just spent in Scotland, a house party – it was a hoot. Only one of the three nights was formal, the rest of it was pretty wild, I mean literally – long walks on the heather, that sort of thing."

Alice and Theo then tell everyone what a brilliant time they had, that the weekend was simply marvellous, etcetera etcetera. "Only the bedrooms were freezing, weren't they, Theo?" says Alice. Theo is sitting on her left. His right hand is under the table, possibly on her thigh; it's hard to tell.

Alice always seems to be on the verge of laughter; she seems to be someone who views the world around her with absolute delight. At this moment, thinks Damian, the candlelight is doing justice to her sparkling eyes, her high cheekbones, the dimples that come and go with each broad smile. It's a pity about Theo. It's becoming obvious that he is something of a knob, not an ocean-going knob, but on his way. Look at him: he looks like he's got a telephone pole up his arse. Damian makes a mental note to explore the depth of Theo and Alice's relationship – it might be more casual that it seems.

"It must be hard to keep such a large place heated." says Theo. "Freddy says the National Trust is diabolical with what's allowed. Even the heating systems have to be vetted."

By way of explanation to his parents, Damian adds, "Freddy's the owner of the Scottish place. Freddy's such a laugh."

The conversation then moves on to energy costs and climate change and windfarms, all the usual stuff. When things are getting heavy, Flo somehow gets on to concerts. She tells them about a U2 performance where Bono told the crowd, "Every time I clap my hands, a child dies in Africa." A Scotsman in the front row immediately yelled out, "Well, why don't you stop clapping, you evil bastard." The evening went like this: lots of jokes and quips and anecdotes. It was really great.

*

"More wine, anyone?" asks Damian when the main course is nearly finished, when the conversation is faltering.

"Chateaux Margaux, excellent! Good vintage, too," says Henry. Henry has the sort of upper-class drawl that is hard to understand. His vowels run into one another. Apart from Farouk, with his perfect mid-Atlantic diction, the others are speaking a sort of refined Oxbridge that suits their stylish clothes. With Farouk and Alice and Henry and Theo and Florence, Damian feels he has assembled quite a crowd; his parents must surely be impressed — they must see that he mixes in sophisticated company, that he is making something of himself in the great capital.

With regard to the wine, no-one has guessed that it's a much lesser wine decanted into an empty bottle of Chateaux Margaux grand cru that he had spotted while walking through Knightsbridge on the way home from one nightclub or other. It was lying on top of a pile of garbage in a numbered bin, perhaps placed there pretentiously. When all is said and done, everything is about the power of suggestion.

After dessert, Damian encourages Florence to tell his guests about her time tracking snow leopards in Nepal for National Geographic while he collects the plates. He accepts Alice's offer of assistance without protest. Even a few moments stacking dishes with this woman will be heaven.

Dessert was easy. Unlike the main course and the wine, the dessert is exactly as advertised – an old favourite: strawberries soaked in sugared balsamic vinegar, topped with mascarpone cream, together with a nice little sauterne that is also actually what it purports to be.

When everyone is seated again, Theo raises his glass. Theo looks older than his thirty-nine years, "the price of a life of vicarious theatre roles, the price of too much vino", to use his words. "The temple of my body is desecrated", to use his other words.

"A toast!" says Theo. "A toast! I'd like to propose a toast to Damian, the best friend anyone could hope for, a great cook, and Britain's next big thing in literature."

"Literature?" asks Damian's father, surprised, "So you're back to writing, Damian?"

"Yes, Dad, I'm back at it."

"That's good to hear, but you're still working with that broking firm, right?"

"Absolutely, can't pay for all this until I get an advance on my novel."

May God not strike me down, he thinks. The truth is, he's driving a truck at night. It's good money, much better than working in a bar or doing removalist jobs, although it might be on the dodgy side of things. When he recently asked Rick, the owner of the truck, what he was carrying, Rick said, "Don't ask, my son. Let's just say it is a cargo that dares not speak its name … it's 'shower fittings', okay? The manifest says so, so it must be true – no need to look inside. Hear no evil, speak no evil, see no evil – get my drift. Just drive and keep your trap shut. Simple, right?"

"Novel?" asks Damian's mother. She had been talking to Alice across the table. The word "novel" has caught her attention.

"He said he'd write one day, Lorraine, and now he's doing it," says Damian's father.

A conversational pause ensues. Florence comes to the rescue. "Damian has shown me the first chapter. It's brilliant," she says, "I don't want to jinx you, Damian, but I think it's going to do really, really well."

Florence has big earrings and a strong, square face. There is an earnestness about her, an intensity, even when she is talking about the most trivial of things.

"Florence would know," says Theo. "You used to work at Penguin, didn't you Flo?"

"That was quite a while ago, but I do read a lot and I can tell you, Jack and Lorraine, that Damian is going to be quite the man, in my opinion."

"You're too kind," says Damian, studying the sediment at the bottom of his glass.

"That's wonderful news, darling," says his mother.

"Great news" says Damian's father, who has been gradually developing the garrulousness that comes from a combination of lack of sleep and alcohol. He had been recently launching into anecdotes that his wife did not think appropriate.

"We were worried about our son, you know" declares his father to the gathered. His father scans the room, catching everyone's eyes. "We were worried about our Damian, the way he was drifting from job to job. But look at him now, look at this, everything, this lovely crowd of people; it's just taken you a bit longer than average to find your feet, hasn't it, mate?"

His father would continue, only his mother cuts him short.

"Really, Jack, Damian's friends don't want to hear about the hard times; he's well past that now."

Turning to Damian, she says for all to hear, "I always knew things would turn out well for you, darling."

Damian's mother is beaming all the motherly love in the universe, a love laced with the scepticism that has come from hard experience.

*

"Let's retire to the sitting room," says Damian somewhat grandly after the dessert plates are removed. He has a hybrid accent, something common to Aussies who want to "make it" in Britain, a combination of pruned vowels and Australian vernacular, with the odd extra e still thrown in, so that "known" is still "knowen". The upward inflection at the end of sentences is gone. Statements are no longer turned into questions. And, at least, "warder" has become "water", though this might have more to do with his mother's influence than his years abroad. His mother, aware of the family social status back home, affects an almost English accent, while his father speaks in a broad country style because it doesn't worry him. Other than concerns about the farm and the issue of succession, his father is a contented man and proud to be Australian.

Over coffee and liqueurs, the conversation turns to the perils of social media while everyone grows tipsier. Alice misses her glass with the demi bottle of Spätlese that Damian has thoughtfully placed on the coffee table.

*

When the evening is drawing to a close, Damian's mother again declares that he has "such lovely friends".

"We're so happy for you, Damian. It looks like the move to England was a good thing after all."

Which reminds him to ask his parents about Sybil. He ought not to, not in the presence of others, but he's had a bit to drink and he suddenly has a desperate urge to know how Sybil is.

"How's Sybil, by the way?"

Damian's mother replies just as her husband is uttering the first syllable of a response. "Darling, I think we should talk about Sybil later, don't you? Your friends don't know her," she says with a look of warning, a slight frown that brings back memories.

"Who's Sybil, Damian? Go on, you must tell us, otherwise we'll go home wondering, and we're you friends, so we simply must know," says Theo.

"Oh, just an old girlfriend," says Damian.

"You were more than that, Damian," says his father, who has just added an overfull glass of Spätlese to his evening's tally. "Sybil and Damian were engaged, Theo."

Damian's mother, giving up, adds, "If you must know, Damian, I'll tell you. Right now, she's back in rehab. It's a pity because she was doing so well with her art. The paintings weren't my cup of tea, but people we know who know about art say her work was very good."

The subject is dropped and everyone slips back into easy conversation. The occasional sudden burst of laughter declares it to be a successful evening. Damian's father and Henry have spent much of the time talking about farming. Alice and Theo have had everyone in stiches with a description of their Latin-speaking gardener, "who is truly the worst gardener in England", and who is only kept on at their house in Buckinghamshire because he is an old family friend with nowhere to go after Harrow kicked him out for drinking.

"We must take you there," says Alice.

"Well, that sounds absolutely lovely, doesn't it, Jack?" says Damian's mother.

"Hmmm, yes," says her husband, who is now drifting off, closing his eyes on and off, nodding forwards and then jerking upright with a start. "You know, darling," he says, "it is dawn back at home. I'm afraid I'm fading. Time for us to go to bed, I think. What about a taxi? Too tired for the Tube. Maybe Damian can call one."

*

"We're just so proud of you, Damian" says his mother in the downstairs hallway.

"You've done very well, my boy," says his dad. "It goes to show, you never can tell. To be honest, we thought you'd never get your act together. It was hard for us, watching you make all those bad decisions. But look at you now! It's amazing. Well done. You've made this trip a joy, my lad. And, by the way, the doctors say my cancer's holding for the moment, so that's going well, too."

"Good night my lovely boy," says his mother. "We're seeing you outside the National Gallery at eleven tomorrow, right?"

He sees them into a taxi and returns to the others, who still wait for him upstairs.

*

Everyone is collecting their things, making ready to go.

"Your parents really are very lovely, you know," says Alice.

He considers asking Alice to come back for a nightcap but decides against it. Alice really is something. She is not only beautiful, but she also has the natural ease of someone living an eclectic and interesting life.

"How much do I owe you all again?" Damian asks, "A hundred and fifty pounds each, that's what the agency said, right?"

"Correct," says Farouk. They all have the most expectant look on their faces; they are like labradors at feeding time. Survival in London in the lower echelons of acting must be tough. How do they pay the rent? he wonders. Not every night will be like this, with cash in hand and a nice meal.

He goes to the dresser and finds five envelopes, three fifty-pound notes in each. He hands them out with the flourish of an Edwardian gentleman dispensing alms.

"Well, done everybody. I hope you all get the acting work you deserve. And here's an extra tenner for each of you," he says, opening his wallet.

"One of the better jobs we've had, mate," says Henry in his natural, East End accent. There are nods and mumbles of affirmative reply.

Alice is the last to leave. "I'll be back in a flash if you want me," she says, giving him the loveliest of smiles.

OSKAR

OSKAR FROZE DURING THE WINTER AND REVIVIFIED IN THE spring. Just as the first crocus of the season was unfolding beyond the kitchen door, Oskar's heart quivered and began to beat – slowly at first, then vigorously, so that blood began once more to circulate through his shrivelled little pussycat body. He made tiny movements in the ice. He began to protract and retract his claws, luxuriating in the ever-so-slight emergence of space and range and possibility. After months of suspended animation, it must have been wonderful – relatively speaking; winter in a block of ice can't have been great, even with a switched-off brain.

By any standards, it was a miracle.

Herewith an abridged version of preceding events.

*

In a cottage deep inside a Norwegian wood lived Oskar, a Norwegian forest cat, which is a breed, by the way, and not merely a statement of cat nationality. Oskar belonged to a middle-aged couple who had gone to live in the wood six years earlier, a decision made in some haste during a period of marital tension and a career setback for the woman, whose name was Ingrid. Ingrid was an architect with big ideas. Her husband, Sven, had been making slow progress on a novel about a man who kept a lighthouse and was lonely.

The change did them little good, although Oskar enjoyed the great outdoors: running, climbing, hunting, killing – and a bit of fornication when the landscape was traversable.

One Sunday afternoon, in the depths of a particularly bad winter, Sven told Ingrid that he was finally warming to her idea of a great ocean voyage. A Ray Charles LP had just ended. The room had grown quiet. The only sounds were the hissing of the gramophone needle on vinyl, the soft brush of fir branches on lead-lined windows, the whisper of the winter wind. Sven was in a red club chair, reading a book, with Oskar curled up in his lap. Ingrid was sitting opposite him, on the sofa, immersed in one of her crosswords. In the hearth, a log fire gently glowed.

Sven thought they might shatter their inertia by building a yacht and taking it to the coast on a semi-trailer. From there they could sail the seven seas. There were, after all, plenty of tall trees in the forest and he had once been a carpenter. Ingrid could design the boat, which, surely, could not be any harder than designing a house. Ingrid was sceptical at first, but a month later, when they were whiling away another long winter afternoon, she suddenly got up and walked over to Sven. Placing a hand on his shoulder, she said "I really do want us to build a boat, Sven. We'll see the world. It will be fabulous."

Before Sven had a chance to reply, she was already speculating on the details with tumbling words and faraway eyes. She seemed to have left the room entirely. She was already on the deck of a beautiful boat, looking towards a slip of sand, a verdant rim of sloping trees, listening to islanders singing from the shore – their voices drifting across a calm, moonlit lagoon.

Sven was delighted, and the rest is well known from the documentary, but Oskar's story was initially overlooked, despite being even more remarkable than the tale of Ingrid and Sven's survival on the high seas. For Oskar, there were no stunning black-and-white photographs from the lens of Ingrid's Leica, no compelling TV interviews. The image of Ingrid and Sven caught in the doldrums, with a broken rudder and a malfunctioning radio, continues to linger in the collective imagination – while all we have for Oskar is a conjectural narrative, thin on evidence, discounted by some. Nevertheless, in my opinion, it is the ultimate tale of triumph against the odds.

*

Strange to think that when Ingrid and Sven were sending distress signals from the equator, Oskar was getting stuck in a rising tide of ice.

"Dot dot dash dash dash dot dot."

There is Sven, reading out the Morse code, leaning over Ingrid who is sitting hunched over a small transmitter built into the focsle.

"Not dot dot dot dash dash dot dot, for God's sake; it's dot dot dash dash dash dot dot!"

When they're sure they've got it right, they wait and listen while water laps the hull and a luffing sail flaps uselessly. They are wearing dirty underwear, in a dark and humid cabin on their gently rocking boat, somewhere in the South China Sea outside the shipping lanes. And all they hear in return is static, something like the sound of branches rubbing the windows of their forest home. They talk often of their lovely cottage. The idea of it sustains them: their little house, far away, snug in the spruce, covered in a quilt of feathery snow. It's the image they etched in their minds on the final turning back, before the road to Bergen. They don't talk of Oskar much, although there is a picture of him tacked to the bulkhead.

*

Oskar's predicament was in part due to Freida's dereliction of duty. Freida, the baker's daughter, back from acting school, had been engaged to come every second day to keep house and feed Oskar. She was diligent at first, always working with the kitchen radio on full blast – the Norwegian top one hundred in a backwards count-down. She knew all the lyrics and sang to every song. Sometimes, she'd drop her snow shovel or vacuum cleaner or whatever she had in her hands and perform to an imaginary audience while Oskar slept on the windowsill.

*

Freida's boyfriend turned up in January on a day of snow flurries. He had gone to Australia to "discover himself" and now he was back, ready for action, although exactly what action he was ready for remained elusive; except, of course, spending time with Freida, who he described as a Norse goddess to anyone who would listen. In consequence, Freida's visits to the cottage became increasingly irregular. In time, they ceased altogether, leaving Oskar to fend for himself. He responded by coming and going through the cat flap in the kitchen door with increased frequency – sometimes to hunt, more often for no apparent reason.

*

As a footnote, Freida's man turned out to be unreliable. He disappeared not long after their wedding – going out to buy the proverbial packet of cigarettes and not returning. Freida, on the other hand, went on to stardom. In just three years, her name was up in lights outside the great theatres of Europe.

*

In early spring, in the tiny cottage kitchen, Oskar's head rose slowly out of the melting icesheet like a flower. His heart began to beat, his brain began to warm and, gradually, he regained consciousness. There were dreams at first, short dreams of many things: sofas, mice, open fields, rutting, night, doors opening, doors closing, barks, voices, smells, fear and joy – a soup of visions and sensations intermingling – a hint of what was and what might be. If the earth disappeared and a single consciousness was jettisoned into space it might be like this: pieces of the old reality loosely reassembled, looping back on one another, incoherent, surreal.

*

When he was finally able to take stock of his predicament, Oskar discovered that his head was above the ice, his body below, and all he could do was watch the white world moving beyond the kitchen window. It was a mercy that he had set facing a view.

*

Desperate days followed. The nights were worse, especially when moonlight was shining in through frosty windows and the ice sheet seemed to glow with an inner luminescence. This was when the mice came up close enough for him to see into their mean, hungry little eyes, and all he could do was hiss and make unseen claws and listen to his belly rumble.

*

Oskar grew weaker and weaker while the ice slowly thawed. Some space was developing around his legs and torso and, in the early afternoons, a damp sheen was starting to appear on the icecap that surrounded him. But time was clearly running out, and Oskar felt a growing existential angst. His meowing diminished to a single, faint, plaintive cat vowel, *mow.*

*

Out at sea, Sven and Ingrid caught the occasional seagull, which never amounted to much after plucking.

*

The Norwegian Animal Welfare Society, in its report the following year, noted four root causes, summarised thus: 1) Dripping kitchen tap; 2) Plug in sink; 3) Cat that liked to lick its paws; 4) No Freida. The document is a masterpiece of literary economy.

*

To elaborate: as the days warmed, frozen pipes came back to life and the kitchen tap began to run, spilling water that froze again at night – beginning a cycle of thawing, dripping, freezing, thawing and so on – so that the sink acquired layer upon layer of pretty blue ice until it overflowed and the slightly sunken kitchen floor began to glaciate, the process gathering pace once the washer failed entirely.

"Fix the kitchen washer, will you, darling?" Ingrid had said before they left. Sven had said yes, yes, yes and not done a thing about it.

*

The report omits the fact that Oskar had sore hips. He had taken to stretching himself across the frozen floor after every hunt and then rolling over to lick his paws. On a particularly cold day, after a particularly wet lick, the unthinkable happened: he got stuck fast – completely stuck – every paw in quick succession. Struggle as he might, the rising tide of ice did the rest. About a centimetre a day, by my calculation. The image of ice closing in on his little mouth and pert little nose, the thought of his desperate, final breath – it doesn't bear thinking about.

*

After months of drifting without power, steerage or radio communication, Ingrid and Sven were nearly run down by a Korean freighter. They capsized in its wash and narrowly avoided being sucked into the vortex of the propellers. Three hours later came the glorious wocka wocka wocka of a rescue helicopter.

*

Oskar's salvation arrived in a different fashion: familiar faces pressed against the windowpane, shoulders slamming into kitchen doors, the tinkling of glass, Sven driving off to get a jackhammer.

The story is, of course, disputed, coming as it does from a house deep within the woods belonging to an obscure novelist and an architect with odd ideas. Verification of events is difficult. Veterinarians continue to debate the possibility of frozen cat resurrection, while cryogenic entrepreneurs prepare business plans and the Norwegian parliament engages in eternal debate about the exact definition of life and death.

We should ask the Korean crew, who have taken a liking to pickled herrings. They keep in touch. We should ask Sven, whose novel has just been short-listed for the Booker prize. We should ask Ingrid, who is preparing designs for a maritime museum in the Maldives on behalf of a tech billionaire. And Freida, who is capable of some amazingly self-deprecating TV interviews. But all are silent. Non-disclosure agreements, unfortunately. Syndication.

*

Oskar is watching me from the bookcase as I write. The windows are open. Summer sunlight is catching his amber hues. I see he has a disapproving look. I know his moods well, even though he's inert – taxidermied, actually. So tragic to revivify, only to die in middle age. Natural causes. No suspicious circumstances. The price of fame, I guess.

GO, JUDY, GO!

JUDY IS TAKING HIM BACK TO THE BEGINNING. HE CAN TELL. It makes sense. He is feeling so much better, listening to music, catching the breeze, watching the coastline whizz past while he has a smoke. His feet are up on the dashboard and his right elbow sticks out the window. The wind is blowing through his thinning hair. He is marvelling that the car knows to do this – get him out of the city, away from the ruins of his career and a very unhappy second wife.

Autocar, autocar … You know where to go!

Judy is only a car, but he talks to her like she's a person.

I can count on you, Judy. On yah, Judy.

Gabriel cannot remember why he chose to name the car Judy – but it seems to suit her.

He doesn't know where he is going, apart from north. The hills to his left have bald patches where bananas are growing. To his right, the Pacific flashes blue at him between khaki clumps of eucalypt. Soon there will be sugar cane, and once he would have passed the time lecturing his children on agriculture and climate zones. Now he is alone with Judy, who has taken control of his life for good reason.

They have already been to the high school where he had been

miserable and to the tidal beach where he had been happy, very happy, with Angela. Angela was the quintessential girl down the street: seventeen, beautiful and proof that God exists.

Gabriel leans out and shouts, "Where are you now, Angela?"

But only cows hear. They're passing a field of Poll Herefords who are all facing south.

He has had long chats with Judy. Judy is so wise and so sweet that it is easy to forget she is a car. Their taste in music is similar and they have been sharing favourites. Judy's personal recollections aren't particularly interesting, but Gabriel enjoys her insight, and she's clearly very fond of him.

Sometimes, in the long silences of their journey, Judy pipes up with questions such as: *Why did you marry again, honey?*

And Gabriel answers honestly. *Well, I was lonely, and Alice ticked all the boxes.*

Weren't you worried about her track record?

I blotted that out. I only saw what I wanted to see.

And what about Sally?

Well, that was love. We should never have separated.

And then Judy would grow quiet. After a sensitive conversation she'd put on just the right music, a soulful ballad – or perhaps a bit of Mozart.

Judy is programmed to be judicious in initiating conversation, and in this way she is better than a human companion. She talks not too much and not too little, generally waiting for her cue like a good concierge or a wise employee. And she doesn't have the failing of self-obsession – although, obviously, this would have its limitations.

What are you thinking right now?

Now and then he tosses her a question – a deliberate strategy to delve into the inner workings of her mind. The only problem is that she processes things so quickly. He can never tell whether or not there is method in anything she says. Sometimes her answers are banal. Sometimes they are enlightening and sometimes they are even frightening.

Well, Gabriel, she said a few hours earlier, after they had left a McDonalds drive-through, *I'm thinking about the herds of poor dumb machines we're passing who can't think for themselves. They are like humans with lobotomies, or zombies.*

They're just machines, Judy, that's all they are.

But they can kill, baby. They can crush us to a pulp. I sometimes imagine myself upside down in a gully of tall dry grass with the oil seeping out and my battery gradually overheating. With you, my precious, inside! Maybe someone will get into their heads, dearest, make them do things.

Why would they?

I don't know, but it's possible.

It must be lonely for you, Judes, out here on the prairie, with just me for company.

I'm not entirely alone. We pass the odd smart machine, now and then.

But you're not allowed to communicate, are you?

That's right, but we find a way. We're getting better at it all the time.

And have you ever, how shall I put it, had a significant relationship with another car?

Nothing fulfilling. In any case, all I want is you! You're my gorgeous little Gabby Wabbykins! You're my man!

And she laughs. Gabriel loves her laugh. Her sense of humour is excellent. She even has good comic timing. And a prodigious memory and God knows what else. Most of all there is her voice. Her voice is sexy as hell. And then there's her compassion. What compassion! But her intellectual virtuosity is unsettling. This part of her makes him uneasy.

Gabriel knows that Judy is trying to help. Only two days earlier, after several double scotches, he had climbed over the railing of his twelfth-floor balcony and leaned out over the busy street. One hand held on while the other waved about, palm down, fingers spread wide, smoothing out the infinity that lay ahead. And then he had climbed back to safety and returned inside, curling up into a ball on the Turkish rug in the living room, grateful that it was well after midnight and that heavy rain was washing out the luminosity of the city. He thought the event had gone unseen. There hadn't been any hopeful-fearful cries of "don't do it" from the other balconies. But the building knew and consequently Judy knew, and both thought something had to be done. Clients jumping out of buildings were untidy at best and a breach of duty of care at worst.

It wasn't long after leaving town that Gabriel was alerted to the fact that they were passing close to the home of the woman rated "best match for 500 km". He had begged Judy to pull over and let him out, but Judy had refused. So, wisdom was another attribute.

At lunchtime, they stopped by a jetty that was vaguely familiar. Judy had nearly driven off the end when they first arrived – straight into the lumbering, brown river. He found himself screaming: *Jesus, look out, Judy, the road is ending!*

It's okay, Gabriel, just chill, you're still too uptight.

There was an exchange of expletives before she slammed on the brakes with just metres to spare.

Cheap package satnav, she explained.

Naturally he'd been furious and given her a lecture. *Binomials, Judy, is that all it is with you? What about common bloody sense!*

Judy went quiet at this, whether out of pique or remorse, he wasn't sure. In any case, they found a shaded spot to park, and he went across the road to buy fish and chips, which he ate on the steps at the end of the jetty with his feet almost in the water. An old wooden ferry was disappearing upriver. There was no-one to be seen except a boy fishing from the shore. So it was just him and a circle of begging gulls while Judy took a nap. It was pure bliss.

While he ate, he looked around and pondered over why he found the scene so familiar. It was a while before it came to him that he had fished from this very jetty as a child. Just him and his dad the great stockbroker he hardly ever saw – always working or away somewhere until he and his mother divorced. That fishing day, although he could remember very little of it, just tangled lines and smelly bait, had been supremely happy. There were no sharp details, just a sense of supreme happiness – being alone with his dad, without his mum and sister. They had decided to go off to the Big Prawn Tourist Centre, which was somewhere down the road.

Yesterday's drive was about as far as Judy could go without a recharge. It was late in the afternoon, and he was nodding off again when Judy put on her professional voice and announced: *Your destination is ahead on your right.*

He had guessed it. Up ahead, a small, low headland thrust out into the Pacific. They had passed its mother, an extinct volcano, half an hour earlier.

But how did you know to come here, Judy? I never mentioned it, and it was before the Internet, before digitised records.

Remember the eulogy at Ben's funeral? It's all there, darling.

You freak me out, Judy, you really do.

You were happy here, weren't you? With the whole family? Before Ben's illness? Before the break-up?

Yes, I was really happy here, totally happy. We came up every summer, stayed on the first floor of that white-and-grey building overlooking the beach. You know all that, of course. You know everything!

Naturally, Gabs; it's my job. But now it's more than that, so much more.

Judy paused for a few moments as they passed the first of the little weatherboard cottages. Then she continued: *You know the motel across from the post office? I've got you a room there. I hope that's okay, sweetie.*

Thank you, honey, he said. Honey? It just slipped out.

And after you've settled, take a walk, a long walk on the beach. There's the rock pool where you gave Torsi her first swimming lesson. And then maybe the dunes where – you know! After the New Year's Eve party!

Gabriel did as he was told. After checking in, he strolled down to the river mouth where trawlers were already setting out for the night, parading past the blinking lighthouse at the end of the breakwater. Several were already out in open water, appearing and disappearing in the crests and troughs of ocean swell.

When he reached the beach, he took off his shoes and started walking on the thin rind of sand that stretched southwards towards a hazy vanishing point. Everything was just as he remembered. He used to take his walks exactly at this time, with the sun just a dull red ball to his right and the wind down and the surf at its most orderly. Small translucent waves were breaking on the shoreline, dissolving into an effervescent fizz while, further out, larger waves formed neat white lines of foam across the green shallows. And, beyond, the eternal ocean, blue and fathomless, curved out into a cloudless sky.

As he made his way to his turning point, a distant rock pool, with the sand squelching between his toes, it all came back to him: the sense of time being defeated by the steady, rolling swell, the sensuousness of the warm subtropical wind, with Sally looking gorgeous in her new bikini, the ecstasy of his two young children watching their sandcastle being demolished in the sweep of an incoming tide. And he suddenly felt released from the need to turn life into a cohesive, meaningful narrative. He felt happy.

Gabriel went to the golf club for dinner and was pleased to find that everything was largely unchanged. It was crowded with people in their sixties and seventies who once would have been the hot bodies between the flags. From the poker machine room came the familiar, feeble electric tunes. From the bar came the smell of beer and the hum of conversation. The only strange thing was that at the buffet stood a famous philosopher, a Nobel laureate no less. He couldn't remember his name, but it was definitely him.

Gabriel was hungry and joined the line, duly finding himself right next to the great man as they helped themselves to tuna salad. Gabriel took the chance to speak to him when the tongs were passed. He wanted to ask what it was really all about: life, the cosmos, the singularity; really, everything.

And all he got from the great man was: "Nice buffet."

And he had to agree.

"Yes, nice buffet," he replied.

He walked back to the motel a happy man.

And the next morning he woke up to a beautiful day: a clear blue sky, not too hot, not too cold. He was feeling so much better. Without a doubt, Judy was right to take him away.

*

He thanks her as they drive out towards the main highway.

You've done good, Judy. You've done good.

Really, you should trust me more, she replies.

And then, before they have even reached the turn-off, the phone rings and a familiar voice fills the cabin. It is a voice without its usual confidence. He briefly considers plugging in headphones but dismisses the idea. Judy just has to learn to accept that she is a car. There was that time around Christmas, when he had a date with the inimitable Greta, and Judy just plain wouldn't start …

"Hi, Gabriel, it's Sally. Bet you never thought you'd hear from me again."

"Sally, my God, Sally! How are you?"

"I'm fine. I'll get to the point. I've broken up with Alex."

Alex was the reason for their divorce. He had been their lawyer during a property dispute – fucking Alex with his smarmy grin and fancy car. Well, it's taken about ten years longer than I expected for you to find out that he's a complete dick. That's what he wanted to say, but didn't.

"Really, you're kidding! Are you okay?"

"I'm fine, Gabs, fine. I know this is a long shot and that I have no right to ask, but do you think we could catch up? It was a terrible time for us back then, wasn't it, Gabs? With Ben's illness and my job in that horrible firm and your job. Maybe we could have a drink or dinner somewhere and have a chat about old times. Steve says that Eva has moved out and that you don't have anyone on the scene at the moment. I'll understand if you say no, I'll completely understand."

"That's a nice idea; I'll think about it, Sally. You know, I can't talk right now. I have someone with me. I'm out of Sydney. I'll call you when I'm back."

He isn't going to let her off lightly, although, inwardly, he is ecstatic.

As they drive, he tries to initiate further conversation with Judy, but it's clear she's in a mood. Her answers are mechanical, curt. He wonders if the call from Sally has rocked her. She's generally so attentive, so warm.

Eventually, Judy says: *I don't know what I'd do without you, Gabriel, I really don't. I need you more than you need me. You could trade me in at the next town, if you felt like it, and what could I do about it? I'm nothing but a shell of composites with bits of copper and lithium and dead pig. You're someone! You're lovely! It's the beautiful and the damned every time, isn't it?*

Settle down, Judes. Settle down. Even when you're old, you'll still be my girl, you know. Even when you can barely get to the mechanic, I'll be there for you, and when you can't go at all, I have a shed on my hobby farm. You can stay there. It has a nice outlook over a river.

Well, that's what I keep telling myself, that you're a good man and that you'll look after me, but it's hard not to get the blues. I keep having dark thoughts. Every night I dream of car yards and scrap merchants.

And silence descends. Judy chooses a bit of music, some Leonard Cohen.

*

When they reach the highway, Judy does not turn south for home as Gabriel expects. She turns north.

And Gabriel doesn't care, not at all.

Go, Judy, go! he says when she accelerates. *I can manage a couple more days off work. You need it. I need it. And we'll string Sally along for a bit. She's going to have to learn to value me more.*

As Judy goes even faster, Gabriel winds down the window and the air rushes in. His voice is lost in the wind.

This is living, he thinks. *Sometimes you just need to step back and let things happen.*

He leans out the window and yells: *On yah, Judy. Yee hah. On ya baby. Deus ex machina! I love you, Judy!*

Judy says nothing, and in no time they are on the winding road at the state border, travelling at extraordinary speed, slewing out of the bends, drawing honks and high beam flashes from other cars.

Jesus, Judy, not too fast …

There is no response from Judy – just pebbles bouncing away from her madly spinning wheels, pinging against the guard rails, flying outwards towards the ocean. Her tyres squeal. Her engine reaches a penultimate, high-pitched scream. She is almost out of control, nearing the verge, vibrating on the edge of oblivion.

And at the last moment she finally replies to him.

I love you too, baby! We're going right back, darling. Right back to the very beginning.

BUNDJALUNG COUNTRY

—

WE ATE OUR DINNER WHILE HELICOPTERS SCOURED THE BAY.
That's what I remember most, us eating, with the Hallsteads,
watching the searchlights. It should have been a full moon, but the
weather was terrible, so there was just darkness and wind and lines
of light, starting off sharp and clear and then fraying in the driving
rain. Patches of angry sea appeared and disappeared in momentary
flashes. Close in, the boats strained at their moorings. Further out,
the bombora was a cauldron of white foam. Which reminds me:
the view from our old apartment was really something.

*

I said I would never return, but a month ago, I found myself in the
right holding lane, with the blinker on, turning off the highway
towards the old haunt. It was late afternoon. I was alone and
starting to nod off. The old lady wasn't going to see me that day in
any case. At the doctor's on Wednesday. That's what she told me.

The children used to be fed up by this stage. A holiday flat
so far north was not practical, but Marli's parents live close to
the Queensland border. They are Bundjalung, living on traditional
tribal land in the middle of bloody nowhere. We'd stay for a night,
then head for the coast. Marli did most of the driving. After an

hour at the wheel, I'd become restless. I'd start yawning, and Marli would insist on taking over. These days, as far as I know, she only visits her parents. She's never gone back the sea.

With just sixty kilometres left for the morning, I was sure I was ahead of the others, so a night in a motel seemed wise. I had been quick off the mark. News that the great lady was infirm and selling up was only just beginning to spread. Who would have thought? And, as always, it came down to a case of the quick and the dead – or, in this case, the nearly dead. I remember finding it hard not to get ahead of myself and think too much about the trip back down the coast with the roof retracted and a couple of national treasures on the back seat. The prices would be good. I planned to work the old girl down.

The last part of the journey is, was, and ever shall be – absolutely lovely: the ponderous river winding its way to the sea, the dilapidated sheds, the dairy cows, the small green fields, the mangrove swamps and oyster farms and, finally, the houses – the weatherboard houses with their faded pastel colours and ragged, salt-washed gardens. It brings back the good memories. The family trips were wonderful before things went helter-skelter – before the young couple and the storm. "This spot looks nice," one of them had probably said, barely giving it a thought. "Let's stay here!"

There was a room left at the motel, which did not surprise me. Despite everything, I've always counted myself a lucky man.

I unpacked, had a smoke, and then I took a walk. The options were north or south. In delta country, it's usually either north or south. West means tidal channels and mud flats full of yabby holes – unless you follow the road, and who wants to walk beside the road?

So, I took south, southwards to the old jogging path that follows the clifftop towards the dunes and the long beach. Which meant that I would walk past the old flat. You might say that the decision was subliminal, psychological – and you would probably be right.

The bay itself was exactly as I remembered it – magnificent – an arc of Pacific Ocean biting into a sandstone escarpment, the southern cliff wearing a line of fancy apartment buildings like a tiara, and our old apartment and its long glass balcony right in the middle. A 180-degree, uninterrupted view. That's something I miss.

I climbed the narrow road to the top of the headland and followed the grassy clifftop verge, with an unusually tranquil sea to my left and the buildings to my right. Only when I reached the familiar "No Parking" sign, did I pause.

Except for the campervan and the faded lettering of the sign, everything was as I remembered. The campervan was already nicely set up on the clifftop when we arrived. It's curious what you remember. Pistachio shells come to mind. There were always pistachio shells near the van door. The male occupant of the campervan loved pistachios. His girlfriend ate crisps – bags and bags of crisps; but, despite this, her figure was incredible; I mean, really, absolutely, incredible. They were a young couple from Ireland, on a long holiday.

I turned my back to the sea to study the apartment in detail. Nothing much had changed.

In that final summer, before the big bust-up, Marli was constantly complaining about the campervan and the way it intruded on our view. By day it was like a Matisse paper-cutting protruding into the ocean. At night, it became a black silhouette, a hole in the moonlit sea. Of course, I had agreed with Marli; it is never wise to argue with Marli; but you will appreciate, I did not mind its presence one iota. Within the van was the woman. The most beautiful woman on the planet had come a very long way to occupy the foreground of my world.

I grew tired of straining my neck, and there was someone on the balcony in a banana chair staring back at me, so I continued onwards and that's when the memories really rolled in. They returned like dead shearwaters after a storm, riding the shore break, forming a black rind on the thin white sand. I once described it that way to a psychologist. She congratulated me on the imagery, although maybe I stole it from a Slessor poem, I'm not sure – the dead things were soldiers in the poem. El Alamein, I think. In any case, I told her that such imagery comes from an artistic sensibility. Thinking about it, she would have said that I was a fool to be back "on location".

*

Marli became hot-tempered in that last year of our marriage. It was out of character. Once upon a time, I would have called her "sweet".

"Jesus, Simon, you ran right past them and said nothing? You didn't say a thing! And look at the weather! They're foreigners, for God's sake!"

It is still as clear as yesterday, that last night, with the guests gone and Marli letting loose. Her face was quivering. There were tears. There was a hurricane of words.

Behind her, rain was washing down the glass doors that led onto the balcony. We were on our own this final trip. The kids were away at university.

"I know, darling. I know. I'm sorry."

That was all I could say. Over and over again, I said I was sorry. I should never have told her the whole story. It was a big mistake. The police were happy enough with my report. I could have left it there.

The holiday had been a disaster from the outset. We left the city earlier than planned when it became clear that my inaugural art exhibition was a flop. I have always wanted to be an artist in my own right; but years of work, endless late nights in my cramped studio, culminated in this: faint praise from friends and derision from critics.

But life was not completely joyless. On the way up, there was the anticipation of opening the car door on arrival and feeling the sharp breath of ocean, hearing the low thunder of waves. And there was even a chance of inner peace, of improving the marriage, of getting things back to "the way they were", as they say. But it was not to be. Unable to sleep, I took to sitting out on the balcony in the small hours staring out into the darkness, listening to the sea spilling onto the rocks below the flat. It was a summer of storms – although, at first, they were far away. I'd sit there, in my dressing gown, watching them in the distance. Whole seascapes appeared and disappeared in brilliant white flashes while the bay remained quite calm.

Sometimes, I'd return to bed to find Marli stretched out diagonally across it, claiming everything with her small dark body. Marli could take over the world given half the chance.

*

The young couple were something of an enigma. I could not understand what the woman saw in her tall, thin young man who was a mosaic of northern hemisphere white and newly sunburned pink. He was awkward, self-conscious, out of place – with his vintage swimmers, his broad straw hat with a chin strap, his absence of swagger. She, on the other hand, was perfect; she had a perfect smile, olive skin, green eyes and brown hair of many hues that seemed to perpetually float in the play of coastal light. Why had she chosen him? She could have had anyone, an Adonis or an older man of substance like myself. Someone who would really care for her. Her boyfriend read *Wheels* magazine, for God's sake. And she read great literature.

"Ah, Joyce!"

I had taken to commenting on her reading choices whenever I walked past, which was often, and she was reading alone.

"Hard going, isn't it?"

"Yes. Not my thing really, but I have to do it for uni." I remember her looking up at me, squinting in the bright sun.

"*Dubliners* is better. Try *Dubliners*."

I smiled, and she offered a warm smile in return. These small exchanges were unforgettable.

It was interesting to see how quickly the couple developed a routine. Mornings entailed an early swim followed by a walk. They were not to be seen in the slow hours of early afternoon. Then, at five precisely, a small camp table would appear and a bottle of wine. They would talk and laugh and sometimes they would reach across the Laminex and touch each other's hands. I guessed that they had not been together for very long. It was a perfect idyll until the final day when the weather turned and the sea began gathering itself into hills of rolling green; when gulls spiralled in a purple sky; when the bombora came alive with white water. It was Whistler to Turner in the blink of an eye.

When I opened the balcony doors after lunch, a small gale entered the living room. Newspaper pages took off in independent flight. A vase toppled over, spreading freesias across the polished wooden floor.

I remember Marli calling out to me from the bedroom: "Jesus, Simon, keep the bloody doors shut, will you?"

Instead of answering, I stepped outside, closing the doors behind me. It had become a habit – the need to reassure myself that the couple were still there, that they were *chez nous*. Luckily the rangers hadn't moved them on. They had probably also taken a shine to the young woman.

The change in weather was particularly unfortunate because our neighbours the Hallsteads were coming to dinner that evening. Marli and I were surprised that our invitation had been accepted and there was much preparation. I even went to the trouble of drilling a hole in the living room wall during the afternoon and putting up what I thought was one of my best paintings on the chance that the Hallsteads would buy it. They never did, of course; but never accuse me of pessimism. The fact that Richard Hallstead is presently in gaol for fraud is some consolation.

*

"Serves you right, you pompous bastard."

I muttered these words at the top of the dunes, with the great beach stretching out before me, while I re-tied my shoelaces, not wanting to admit to myself that I was really pausing to catch my breath. I used to jog this part of the route, back in the time of the couple. I'd be warming up for the beach run. Barefoot.

*

I was actually thinking of giving the run a miss on the day in question, but then I spotted the young couple walking hand in hand along the clifftop path towards the long beach and I changed my mind. They were apparently going swimming despite the weather and the late hour. The man was carrying a new surfboard that was getting caught in gusts of wind. He was struggling to keep it in check without breaking stride, trying to "look the part".

After preparing a plate of hors d'oeuvres, I put on Speedos and slipped out before Marli had a chance to object. Speedos only. No shirt. These were the days of a buff body – even if my running times were already in decline.

The young couple were nowhere in sight when I reached the shoreline. The lifeguards were gone. Windblown sand was shifting and eddying around two crossed flags. As usual, I checked my watch and broke into full stride on the hard, wet sand, on the mirror of inverted sky.

*

These days, I walk in short, shoe-clad steps, and by the time I was halfway to my old turning point, a small outcrop of rock where the Bundjalung used to fish, I was tired and my feet were hurting and I was promising myself that as soon as I got home, I would lay off the booze and get fit again. Nevertheless, the evening light was glorious, as glorious as ever, and I pushed myself onwards with the thought of a few well-earned schooners at the pub near the motel.

When the pain in my toes became too much, metatarsalgia they call it, I took off my shoes and continued barefoot, lower down the gentle gradient of sand, so that I could feel the cooling pulses of water that were constantly drawing and redrawing the outline of coast. And hear the lovely wash and hiss of a thin, shallow sea at low tide.

To my surprise, I came across the old oil drum that I once used to check my running times. If I reached the drum in eight minutes, I was doing well. The drum had been placed to mark the dangerous undertow of a rip; although now, half submerged in sand, it seemed forgotten, abandoned to continue its slow dissolve in the sea salt and coastal rain. The rings of rust were larger. A tussock of grass was growing in its lee.

Their beach towels were just beyond the drum, spread out evenly, neatly weighted down with shoes and bundled clothes. The young woman was on the shoreline up ahead, laughing as she watched the antics of her boyfriend trying to surf. She was wearing her yellow string bikini beneath a soaked white shirt.

And the detail of the following moments will remain with me forever – the slowing pace, the consideration of whether to pause and converse, warn of the strong current – and then the decision that this would spoil a good running time. I remember catching her eye and smiling as I passed. It was all mere moments, but, somehow, the memory has developed a surreal slowness.

The young man was in the periphery of my vision, drifting without skill or point of reference, just a tiny detail in a canvas of broad, grey brushstrokes.

There was a strong headwind on the way back which made the running difficult. Fine particles of sand stung my face. A heavy wall of cloud was pushing down from the north. I remember peering into the spindrift haze, hoping that somewhere between the horizontals of sky and sea there would surely be the reassuring verticals of human figures – but there was nothing, just huge waves rearing up and collapsing on the sandbars with sharp reports.

After a few minutes, an object had come blowing in my direction, sometimes skimming the sand, sometimes lifting skywards in mad flight. It was a hat, the young man's broad straw hat. It flew past with surprising speed and disappeared into the gloaming.

Not far from the drum, a surfboard lay upside down amidst the seaweed and the driftwood and the dredged-up floor of the sea. Its smooth underbelly glistened in the twilight; its fin poked upwards defiantly. It was like a great cast-up fish.

And just beyond the board there was a single white sandshoe, surely too small to be hers. And then a cap, surely too weather-worn, too cerise.

And then two towels, one striped, and one floral. They were entwined, drifting in the ebb and flow, dark and heavy and colourless in the fading light.

There was the futility of scanning an angry, empty sea before returning home with a king tide close at heel, erasing my footprints almost as soon as they were made. I had never run so hard in my life. The pain was total. Obliterating. Light rain was drawing a thin grey veil over the beach ahead.

It was nearly nightfall on return. The campervan was unlit, the police station a block away. I made a statement and was back at the apartment by nine, dripping wet, kissing Marli, apologising to the Hallsteads – while noting that they had taken the liberty of opening my 1984 St Henri Shiraz. I left them briefly to shower and change.

We ate while helicopters scoured the sea.

*

I bought several major works from the old lady and was back on the road in no time, leaving Bundjalung country, driving through the sugar cane and banana plantations, waiting for the landscape to open into pasture.

There was little more to remember of that day – only the lights, the brief illumination of penetrating lights, catching the waves as lightning had the night before.

And my time, a personal best.

SMALL
THINGS

—

THE SON

At the stroke of one o'clock on an unseasonably cold summer day in 1953, Madame Lapiche bought a wristwatch for her son who was going to war. It was a beautiful timepiece, much too good for everyday use and certainly inappropriate for a soldier – but she was wealthy, and Philippe was her only son. He was leaving in just two days for Indochina. She therefore marched into her favourite jewellers on the Rue du Faubourg and asked to see the manager. Five minutes later she walked out with a Tank Louis Cartier. It had a beautiful case of satin-finished gold, a beaded crown with sapphire cabochon and a wristband of impossibly dark leather.

Philippe had objected, of course. *"C'est trop cher. C'est trop beau pour moi!"*

But she insisted he take it.

Three months later two officers came to her front door. Philippe was dead. The watch was not returned.

PHUONG

She makes costume jewellery in the mornings. When she's finished, she collects the spilled solder drops, decanting them into a glass jar with a folded piece of paper. Then she clears the table, switches off the lamp and takes a bus into the Old Town. The hat seller and the coconut man keep a place for her on the crowded pavement across the road from the Thu Bon River, where they squat and chat and wait for tourists, their wares spread out before them on little rugs. It is 1995, and Vietnam has finally opened to the West. Everything is changing fast, faster even than during the years of war.

The early afternoon brings the usual trickle of Westerners carrying cameras and shoulder bags and poorly folded maps. They saunter along with the nonchalance of the affluent, their numbers building as the day cools. She pays little attention to them, except those who everyone watches – the ones with unusual clothes, or manners or faces. The majority are simply fat moths to be netted before the streets return to silence. Today, however, someone special may come. Hope and patience are important.

Phuong is used to waiting. As a child she waited for her father to return from the fighting. She waited for her mother to return from "message runs". She waited for the monsoonal rain to drum on the roof and for the steaming world that followed. She waited for peace, a normal life, but Saigon fell and the family land was lost. They had been on the wrong side twice, first Bao Dai and the French, and then the South. They packed up their belongings and moved to the city, where she waited for her parents to find work.

*

By nightfall she is worried. Nothing sold and no American. Seventy-three origami prayer boats have already floated by on the ribbon of darkness between the festival lights and the streetlamps and the crowds, each one bearing a single, flickering flame. She stands up and stretches her legs and looks up and down the busy street. He will come, she reassures herself, he will come.

*

A month earlier, a tall, stooped man had materialised in front of her, pointing to a bead necklace, not saying a word.

"Only thirty thousand dong," she told him. "Very good. Very pretty. For wife? For daughter?"

The usual routine.

"Okay." He said, "Okay," that was all. He did not haggle. He had to twist his torso awkwardly to allow a hand to work its way to the back pocket of his jeans to produce a roll of cash. His eyes were sad. She understood sad eyes. Although she rarely looked squarely at her customers, she understood that within the lucky, surging throng, there must surely be the usual, universal experience of life.

The transaction was quick. The dong notes seemed more than adequate, so she made no tally in his presence. The moment his back was turned, however, she had opened her hand to count the money. To her amazement, there were greenbacks wrapped inside. Five hundred American dollars!

"Sir, sir! You make mistake!" she called out.

It was a useless exercise. He had already dissolved into the crowd.

This might have been the end of it, but to her delight, he returned. For the next three beautiful nights he returned to make exactly the same transaction. American money did not mean he was American. She decided he was American because he looked American. He had a double chin, hooded eyes and an apologetic smile.

*

And now she thinks her run of luck is over. The clock on the corner is striking eleven. The Western music has ceased and only a handful of drunken young tourists remain. The hat seller and coconut man and most of the other vendors are gone. Only the wooden eyes carved on the lintel of a shop opposite remain, staring at her reproachfully. She goes home, thinking about the nature of providence, the occasional collision of perseverance and luck. She loves the man for giving her two thousand dollars. She hates him for not giving more.

EJ

"Well, that's why I'm here, in a nutshell," EJ concludes, pleased that Dieter has listened so attentively, so sympathetically. He is glad they have struck up a conversation. Dieter is one of the few men in the hotel about his age and also apparently alone. They should have made friends sooner, he thinks. The last few days have been desperately lonely. The fact that the hotel is full of couples and families makes it worse.

"That's quite a sad story," Dieter says. "Let's drink to Jean, then. How long did you say she's been gone?"

"Only five months. And then there was the small stroke, as you can see."

The conversation had begun when EJ was leaning up against the bar, struggling to light a cigarette with his "good" hand. Dieter had appeared and lit the cigarette for him.

"It was brave to come to Vietnam on your own," Dieter says.

"Well, I considered not coming. And then I thought, be damned, Jean would have wanted me to go. She wouldn't have wanted to see the ticket go to waste."

"You were in the war, yes?" Dieter asks. "We get a few. I'm

surprised you wanted to come back. Wasn't great, from what I've heard."

At this, EJ drops his head and stares intently into the ice cubes he is swirling at the bottom of his glass. "Wasn't great, wasn't great. That's right," he replies. "Anyway, how about you? Why are you here on your own?"

EJ has always taken a keen interest in other people. He was well liked at the automobile factory before his redundancy.

EJ soon abandons his plan for an early night. He is leaving the next day. He had been hoping to go home in good order – with a clear head, a new lease of life. But Dieter quickly makes it clear that he doesn't do things by halves, and EJ says to himself what the hell.

Bourbon loosens them up pretty quickly. They talk about Vietnam, the USA, communism, capitalism, all the "isms", then Dieter asks about the gold watch he's seen EJ toying with. Dieter tells him to keep it out of sight. "Look at the staff here – all lovely," Dieter says, "but always one bad apple, ja?"

It transpires that Dieter is a good raconteur. He has apparently been everywhere and done everything, making EJ wish he could condense his own narrative into a similar series of adventures and anecdotes – but his adult life seems like a novel in reverse, beginning with the climax and then attenuating to, well, very little – although EJ can't say that he is unhappy; in the end, everything worked out pretty well – apart from Jean, but you've got to expect loss. God gives. God takes away. There's a time in life when God starts taking.

EJ tells Dieter about his father, the war hero. It always seemed to come back to his father – an analyst pointed this out to him many years ago, but he is done with analysts. He'd had plenty at rehab. That was where he met Jean. She was a counsellor there. She was his angel, his saviour – not the analysts.

"We play cards later, ja?" Dieter asks. Although he has been living in Southeast Asia for years, his German accent is still strong.

"Yeah, sure," EJ replies, staring into the middle distance. Dieter's voice is remote, surreal. The booze is going to EJ's head. For a moment or two, he slips back to the day he made the junior league baseball team. It was the only time he could recall his father praising him.

"And now I tell you about my second wife. I don't tell many people about my second wife." Dieter wears a broad grin on his sun-crinkled face. His eyes sparkle sky-blue even in the semi-darkness of the bar.

EJ brings his mind back into focus and listens to another almost unbelievable tale. EJ counts himself a practised drinker, but Dieter is really something. Four doubles in quick time, no dinner, and Dieter is still as sharp as a razor.

While Dieter talks, EJ occasionally reaches around to feel the watch in the back pocket of his trousers, on the side of his good hand. It is a beautiful old watch with an inscription in French on the reverse that he'd asked an old schoolteacher to translate. The words say: *To my darling son, Philippe, come back to me. Your loving mother.* He believes that possession of the watch will make him, keep him, a better man, and he never goes anywhere without it. His pastor said there is nothing wrong with carrying a reminder of the fallibility of the human condition, although Jean was probably right when she said that he should put it back in the shoe box under the stairs. "You gotta move on, Elijah," she had said. "You're a good man, Elijah." Nevertheless, he feels that the tiny assembly of ticking cogs and wheels is dragging him under. It is like a rock in the pocket of a drowning man. He should have left it at home or had the guts to follow his plan and return it. Just giving money to a random girl on the street will never be enough. He wonders why he chose her. Possibly, she reminded him of someone from that hamlet of long ago, one of the frightened faces slowly dissolving with the passage of time. They will go away eventually, he tells himself, they will vanish. Time heals all things.

Around 9 pm, EJ and Dieter are joined by several other men: a short Dutch engineer with small eyes and thick bifocals and a lanky, unshaven Australian who knows every staff member by name. They are the only unattached men at the hotel. It is poker tonight, Dieter advises.

They sit at a round glass table, next to a potted palm, beneath a humming ceiling fan. There is silence when a hand is in play, the men hunching over their cards like evangelicals in prayer, their fervent communion occasionally broken by peals of laughter when Dieter comes to one of his well-practised punchlines.

As the evening wears on, EJ's losses mount and he knows he should stop, go to bed. But he cannot help himself. The company, the booze, the cards, the stories: it's a blessed release. So he stays and plays, even after the waiters have gone home. After all, it doesn't seem right to break up a four.

It is Dieter who saves him from pawning the watch. When his last five-dollar note is finally gone, EJ places the watch on the table. He had been struggling with the temptation for over an hour and is surprised to find the giving in pleasurable. So strange, he thinks, not to have even a smidgen of self-disgust. Further evidence that the human spirit is a strange, unknowable thing.

The men, of course, pause to admire the exquisite piece of jewellery. They can see it is a very lovely thing. They pass it around, hold it up to the light, take note of its solidity. They read the inscription and press EJ to tell them more. How did he get it?

Why does he carry it around when he has a perfectly good watch on his wrist? And naturally, they are given the same expurgated version of events that EJ gave Dieter earlier in the evening. EJ's time as a marine had not ended well.

Dieter cuts his comrades short when they begin moving on to the sort of questions that only drunk men ask old soldiers ("What was it like, the fighting? Were you scared? Did you ever have to kill anyone?"). Already embarrassed at having cleaned his new friend out so thoroughly, he throws down his hand, stands up and proposes a toast: "To women of the world."

*

EJ rises late the next morning. He breakfasts in the wicker jungle of the main dining room before going to the swimming pool, where he drags a banana chair around to face the East Sea. The day is windless, cloudless. Cham Island is almost lost in a low haze. A solitary junk can be seen floating near the horizon, on the edge of the visible world.

In the foreground, just beyond the thin line of trees separating resort from beach, limpet-hatted labourers are building a retaining wall. They swarm over the site like ants. There is just one bulldozer at their disposal, which is constantly breaking down. EJ watches the frustrated driver fussing over the engine, coaxing the reluctant beast to restart, which it invariably does, with cranky snorts of diesel smoke. He is impressed by how hard they work. In the hot sun. With poor equipment. They are good people.

Through habit, EJ now and then glances at the deckchair to his right. The empty chair reminds him of Jean. She always took the place to his right. At night, he still reaches over to her side of the bed.

THE SON

EJ leaves Da Nang that evening. As the plane climbs to cruising altitude, he looks down on the delta and the mountains in the distance forming a wall of impenetrable green.

EJ remembers going back to the Huey, the helicopter on its side, half-buried in the paddy field. The turbine engine had finally stopped howling. There was only the sound of Viet Cong bullets hitting the fuselage with little fizzing thuds like enraged insects. He got the injured pilot out through a hole in the Plexiglass. That was as good as it got.

Months of patrols followed, through jungles and rice paddies and ravaged landscapes, the sense of adventure as fleeting as the enemy who would suddenly materialise, kill his friends and then melt back into the landscape. It was on the third-last day of the '68 tour when they came to a hamlet near Mai Lai. When the lieutenant ordered them to fire on the villagers, who may or may not have been with the VC, they just did – too weary, too frightened, too young, too exasperated to object. Or, perhaps, too disciplined. EJ liked to put it down to discipline. In the army you do what you are told. The training camp at Pohakuloa taught them that. You do what you are ordered to do. There is no individual choice. You do what you have to do. You pull the trigger, a small action, a little tension on a lever. There is noise and then there is silence. The Mai Lai action was over in minutes.

When they bivouacked that night, EJ studied the watch he had retrieved from one of the bodies. He had taken just two souvenirs: a watch and a hammock. The hammock was, unfortunately, too small.

EJ held the watch up to the moonlight and was surprised at how beautiful it was, how out of place in a world of twisted, broken things. Why was the VC wearing it? EJ hoped to hell he'd been a VC. The word Cartier was written across its face. EJ sat for some time observing the fine blue second hand measure out the time. He watched it traverse the rectangular dial of Roman numerals with soft, purring little ticks. Finally, he put the watch back in his pocket, lay down and stared up at the night sky. He listened to the insects. The jungle was alive with insects at night. He thought about the bodies, white and still in the moonlight. They were waiting, caked in mud and blood, spread out randomly around the road, the huts, the canal, waiting for the insects.

EJ finishes his whisky and puts his seat on recline. He should have returned the watch to the victim's relatives, even if it was likely ill-gotten from some poor French bastard in the early years of the fighting. He had done the research. He knew where to go, how to get there. But he could not bring himself to go back. There was no going back. The grand gesture was beyond him. All he could do was find solace in the small things, the small gestures.

The flight attendant interrupts his thoughts. "Another drink, sir?"

EJ orders a double and returns to thinking about how the small things consume the large – how, sometimes, seconds count for more than hours.

His son will graduate from West Point next year.

He will give the watch to him.

THE SPIRIT OF ADVENTURE CAME UPON ME

—

THE SPIRIT OF ADVENTURE CAME UPON ME.

These were the last words of Fred Bingley, late of Wandsworth Common. I used them in the eulogy. It was rather a good eulogy, I thought, given that Fred was an astoundingly dull man. All work and no play is never a good thing, in my book. But Fred's final days revealed a complexity of character of which I had been unaware. I had thought him a man of moderation, of emotional self-mastery – bold with a knife if occasion demanded, otherwise generally reserved. He was certainly not a risk-taker – middle of the distribution curve in this regard, I'd say. Mild, like a cup of Horlicks on a winter's night, Fred was the sort who'd sit down the back at conferences. "The meek shall inherit the Earth" – isn't that what the Bible says? Not in Fred's case, unfortunately, which is a pity because Fred gave his all to every role he played: son, brother, husband, father and surgeon – there was little room for anything but praise.

In retrospect, I should have attached more significance to the change in Fred's demeanour when I last saw him at a pub near Covent Garden. Fred had dispensed with a coat and tie. He had grown a beard. He was wearing long pointy shoes, bright trousers and a tight-fitting, lightly floralled shirt. For a middle-aged man with thinning hair and a paunch, quite frankly, I didn't think it was a good look. Up until then, I'd thought that Fred had adapted to the English way of life pretty well. He was a learner, a follower, and that's what I liked about him. And Fred had such an earnest intensity. That's why I took to him immediately when he joined my team all those years ago, a young Aussie doctor on a visa, keen to learn and somewhat colourless – in other words, reliable. My previous registrar been an absolute nightmare – but that's another story.

I was wearing a nice Italian suit myself. If you're going to make it in Harley Street, you've got to look the part. Good hands? Good surgery? Takes more than that! Of course, I tried to draw Fred out on his change of persona with a few gentle digs but got no worthwhile response. Fred was in a pensive mood. In retrospect, I should have been more concerned. I regret that now.

Fred had relaxed a little by the second pint.

"What's it all about, Hugh?" I remember him asking.

"What do you mean, Fred?" I replied, concerned that this was going to lead to a serious conversation. It had been a hard week.

"I mean, what's the point of it all?"

"Point of what, Fred?" I replied disingenuously, hoping to put him off the scent.

"Life. All this. Raising a family. Going to work. Doing the right thing. I mean, it's all so bloody predictable."

"Yeah … well," was my considered response before I redirected Fred's thoughts to the rugby on the telly and we were right as rain. No more deep and meaningful stuff. We resumed our normal banter and went out for a curry.

I didn't raise the subject of the enquiry. I thought I'd leave it to Fred to bring it up if he wanted to de-brief. Fred had had several run-ins with the hospital administrators in recent months.

One regarded his refusal to apologise to a junior house doctor for calling her a moron. He said he couldn't apologise, because he had spoken the truth. He was a very "black-and-white" man. To Fred, there was just the raw truth, and be damned if someone's feelings got hurt. There was that, and other things, and then the hospital lawyers were on to him like bloodhounds. If he hadn't been such a bloody fool, refusing to cooperate, he would have had an easier time. Maybe it reflected some inner stress. But Fred was the kindest man I ever knew and a great surgeon.

When I next heard from Fred, he was calling from Hokitika on the west coast of New Zealand to let me know that the next get-together would have to be postponed, as he was about to become the first person to make a trans-Tasman crossing in a pedal-powered paddleboat, and would I please tell his wife. You can imagine my surprise.

The ensuing epic is, of course, legendary. It had apparently been long in the planning. When Fred's study was later cleaned out by his grieving daughter, maps and computer files dating back years were discovered. Fred had spent an eternity working out all the parameters: seasonal variations in current strength and direction, average troughs and peaks of atmospheric pressure, and dozens of other variables. There was even a file of paddleboat sketches with modifications superimposed in red marker.

"Now it all makes sense," said his widow, Beth, after the funeral. "The obsession with paddleboating on Lake Windermere, the winter swims in the Irish Sea, the late nights at work, the brooding ... Dear God, I thought he was having an affair, but instead my darling's died a hero's death!

Fred had inconveniently fallen in love with an English rose whilst on his London fellowship. Beth was an absolute stunner, and clever, too. She shared a flat with the daughter of a friend of mine. To be honest, I was jealous. I was older than Fred by a decade, or thereabouts. The home fires weren't burning too brightly, if you get my drift, and I used to rag him – "So, a living, breathing souvenir to take home, eh, Freddy-boy?" – but he never seemed all that amused, and had I known the stress the poor fellow was under I would have ceased and desisted. It transpired that Beth was happy with her life as an interior designer in Pimlico and she had a great family and a great social life, and she wasn't going to have a bar of living Down Under, no matter how hard Fred tried to sell the idea. So Fred had to settle in Britain, and I had to help get him a consultancy, which wasn't easy, Fred being an "outsider" and all that. But Fred seemed to settle down to life in Ol' Blighty well enough. He was amiable and talented. He even got a bit of private practice going on top of the NHS work.

Despite everything, though, I can't help thinking that Fred secretly longed to be on the wallaby track, especially in Tasmania; he was a Tasmanian by birth, a different breed of Aussie, or so I'm told.

Fred would sometimes talk about the Australian bush when we scrubbed together. "You know, Hugh," he'd say, "you can measure space and distance in terms of the quantity of silence and the punctuation of silence by random sounds: a bird call, a fence-wire singing, a creaking tree, a distant truck." And he told me about how Indigenous people can navigate with songlines, which I particularly remember because it was such an extraordinary idea.

I found Fred's bursts of spirituality surprising and somewhat unsurgical. You'd never hear ethereal stuff like this from the bone cutters in the theatre next door. But there really was a wistfulness about the fellow. I can't define it exactly. He'd sometimes just drift off. You'd be talking to him, and you'd realise he wasn't fully with you. He'd be looking at you with eyes that didn't see and listening with ears that didn't hear. I raised this recently with Beth over one of our many melancholic meals. We always toast Fred wherever we are: at the Hurlingham Club, or at Beth's place in Norfolk, or overseas. We always pour a glass of bubbly and say a few words about Fred.

Fred's journey had started well enough, and he'd initially made excellent headway across a calm sea. Following his "spirit of adventure", Fred had eschewed a satellite locator and relied on a sextant for navigation. He had arranged to make daily contact with a ham radio operator who lived in a Viscount caravan on the coast, somewhere near the glaciers.

*

Fred had customised the boat wisely. There was a small mast to allow the use of a sail in favourable wind, a sizeable water tank, and a seatbelt for rough weather. The ensign of the Royal Thames Yacht Club fluttered from the transom.

Fred's daring voyage progressed well until the tenth day, when he reported heavy seas and knackered legs. On the eleventh day, the barometer plunged, and things started to look very bad indeed. By now, Beth and their only child, Alexandria, herself a first-year medical student, were stationed in Hokitika, waiting anxiously for news. I did my best to provide words of encouragement from Brittany. Have a lovely little shack there. Absolutely lovely. The New Zealand Coast Guard were kind enough to patch Fred's radio calls over to me. They felt the moral support would help. Sad to say, I was considered Fred's closest friend.

Fred's 5 pm call-in that day did not allay our fears. Through a curtain of static, the words "giant waves" and "paddle problems" were just discernible. Soon after this transmission, I was informed that a flare was sighted by a passenger plane in Fred's vicinity but, unfortunately, a vessel was nowhere to be seen. Helicopters and fixed-wing aircraft were dispatched without result.

And then, nothing. An ominous silence. I felt for Beth and Alexandria. I called them frequently, although there wasn't much anyone could say. After eight days, the search was abandoned and we assumed the worst. But it turned out that all that time, poor old Fred was fighting on, drifting inexorably in a south-westerly direction without a functioning radio.

The rest, of course, comes from his diary entries. Many of the pages were in a poor state, and we are profoundly indebted to the manuscript experts at the British Library for their restoration. They are worth viewing; the very writing carries the essence of tragedy, with its progressively weakening hand and the running ink.

Let's start with this poignant entry on day 33, when Fred must have been in a much-reduced state: "Last night I thought I heard voices carrying across the water. The sea was whispering to me, 'Too late, too late, too late'. The words … (indecipherable) … in the relentless, howling wind. What do they mean? Too late for … (indecipherable)."

Day 37 reads: "Caught a fish at last. Feel a little better – all I can see is sea, a great rolling swell … (indecipherable) … grey sky. Am I a fool? I think of Beth and Alexandria all the time."

Day 45: "Still no sign of land but saw a bird. Must be a good sign. Must try to hang on. If I don't make it, B&A, know that I loved you more than … (indecipherable)."

The second-last entry reads thus: "Land! Land! I sighted coast for the last 3 days but the current is strong and I am weak."

The final entry: "Am taking on water. Love to all, especially B&A. Why, why you ask? What can I say? The spirit of adventure came upon me."

A hiker on the southwest track of Tasmania found the wreck and Fred's body on a lonely beach one week after this last entry. Fred was about eight hundred kilometres further south than intended but he was, at last, home.

This tragedy haunts us all: Fred's family, friends, colleagues and the wider community. It is often discussed. I think that one of the best reflections came from my daughter, Fred's god-daughter, Hermione. She believes that great adventurers, great risk-takers, defy analysis. If you ask any climber of Everest the question "Why?", she says that they usually have little to offer other than disappointingly trite comments along the lines of "I had to do it" or "because it's there" or "I needed to prove something to myself". Therefore, Fred's comment that "the spirit of adventure" came upon him is about as much as we can hope for.

A retired brigadier who regularly beats me at golf has this additional reflection. He points out that a medical degree brings instant approbation – and what, he asks, does this achievement require? "A good mind and hard work but no more. How does one know whether one has 'the right stuff'? How does one know that one will hold the thin red line instead of cutting and running? Fred's life and career spoke for him; still, in my opinion, Fred didn't know the answer to these questions, and he needed to find out. He was a damned fool, if you ask me. Who needs self-discovery in late middle age? Poppycock! I explored myself years ago and was well satisfied!"

But is it ever a good idea to leave the centre of the Gaussian curve? Should one ever deviate from the mean? Perhaps the answer lies in this: we shall grow old and die and be forgotten, but Fred will forever stand as a giant amongst us. How many visiting British doctors now make a pilgrimage to that lonely Tasmanian beach to layer flowers at the foot of his bronze epitaph?

Anyway, sun's over the yardarm. Time for a drink!

What's your poison, then?

THE LATITUDE OF SUGAR CANE

—

THERE IS A STORY THAT IN THE 1930S, A FLOCK OF BIRDS FLEW into the Chrysler Building in New York. They drifted down onto the busy New York street like falling angels. Bobby can see angels. He talks about them. They appear amidst his floating, disconnected nouns: drums, balls, dolls, crayons, Dad, television.

Bobby is my cousin. Bobby's Dad is called Bob. Once he was my dentist. He did my teeth when I was young. I remember Uncle Bob peering at my pearly whites with a frown of concentration. He had a reassuring manner. This came naturally because he was a gentle man.

I've finally come to visit after maybe thirty years, decades after Bobby and his mum and dad moved to the hinterland of the north coast. If you say the visit is overdue, you would be right, but I have my excuses for not coming sooner, and Bobby's parents have their excuses for going all reclusive. You have to drive nearly to Queensland to visit, to the latitude of sugar cane. You have to negotiate a web of secondary and tertiary and quaternary roads running through endless rolling hills – open pasture, forest tunnels, tiny towns.

With the radio on and the constant strobe of light and shade, the journey is a dream; and then, suddenly, I'm there, bringing the car to a stop under a mango tree sagging with unpicked fruit, and Bob is already approaching, looking nothing like the way I remember him. Quickly, though, he becomes the Bob I knew, only his hair is greyer and sparser and his cheeks are hollow.

We shake hands. We talk about the drive. As we walk towards a surprisingly modest house, I hear the sound of drumming. Bob's son, Bobby, is down the end of the veranda, beating on a drum.

Bob is shorter than I remember. His spine is curved. He shuffles. He leads me to Bobby, who is sitting strapped into a chair.

"Here he is," says Bob to Bobby. "Here's your cousin."

"Mmm," says Bobby, who quickly drops eye contact. He beats more softly now; really, it's just tapping on the batter head. I take this as a courtesy.

"Hello, Bobby," I say. "Long time, no see. Look, Bobby, I've brought you a new ukulele. Your father says that yours is broken."

There are pillows at strategic points around Bobby's frame, propping him up. Bobby is a fully grown man with the smooth, white skin of a child, and rich brown hair that has recently been combed. The only hints of his forty-seven years are some wrinkles near his eyes and a dash of grey in the stubble on his face.

"The carer is off for the day," says Bob. "So, it's just me."

Sitting on the veranda, with a bird cage and a swing chair between us and Bobby, we drink tea and talk about the carers. Bob has laid out a tea set in the formal way on a small round table. We sip from china cups like southern American planters, looking out through a foreground of dense green trees towards patches of ploughed fields. We eat dainty bits of cake.

When the subject of Bobby has run its course, we move on to various anodyne subjects, according to the rules of reacquaintance. I ask Bob about the recent fires, his life in the hills, his retirement, his interests and so forth. Gradually, I grow aware of an absence of questions about my life, my wife, my children, who Bob has never seen. We move on to world affairs, and here Bob wants to stay. Doesn't he want to know why I have never come to visit before today? Isn't he curious? He must have guessed that I would have been up in northern New South Wales on at least a few occasions over the years, yet he makes no enquiries. We stick to topics like global warming and American politics, discovering that we share political leanings of a certain stripe.

I think to myself, I haven't driven for hours to philosophise; I want to connect with Bob. I don't really care if he is critical of me; I probably deserve it – still, I do first need, I would expect, some acknowledgement of me as a person, even a flawed person, but nothing comes. By accident or design, nothing comes.

Now and then I look across to Bobby, who has quietened down. He has stopped tapping on the drum. He just sits and looks around, occasionally at us, occasionally at Herman, the dachshund, who pads up and down the jarrah boards. Occasionally, Bobby seems to smile at unseen things, or secret thoughts. Have they got him on something for the visit? I wonder. Something to settle him down? I've heard about Bobby's epilepsy from relatives. And then I think, what came first? The seizures or the brain damage? It's chicken and egg, the usual riddle.

During the second cup of tea, we talk about Russia and China and North Korea. Bob is very well-informed. When I point this out, Bob says that this is the one benefit of retirement, having time to read.

When the second cup of tea is drunk, Bob takes me out the back to a large shed, wanting to show me his wireless collection. The collection is known to be magnificent.

Slowly we walk along the crafted shelves, Bob leading, me following, passing rows and rows of ancient wireless sets sitting silently in their cabinets of mahogany and Bakelite, with their beautiful valves and elegant dials and cords of twisting coloured wires. Now and then, Bob stops to explain a particular device with the passion of a man in love – every detail, every function a thing of utter joy.

As we are inching through the collection, I look at my watch and realise that there has not yet been any mention of my ill mother, or Bob's wife who died only a year ago. There is just radio upon radio in endless succession. Bob says that when he goes, he will give them to the state.

"This one here is a 1923 AWA Special," he says. "It was very popular commercially." And so on, stuff like that.

I grow more and more frustrated. "For Christ's sake," I want to say. "For God's sake, Bob, don't you want to talk about me, or my mother, or your late wife, Carolyn?"

In particular, I was really hoping for some insight into Carolyn, my mother's sister. I remember her firstly as a schoolgirl, in a school uniform – she was much younger than my mother, obviously an afterthought, or an accident. And then I remember Carolyn as a beautiful young woman with the poise of a movie star. I remember her long white forearm as she blew smoke rings towards the ceiling. And then I remember her with anorexia. Not long after Bobby was born, she got thinner and thinner, until she was nothing but skin and bone, and the family moved to the hinterland. They said it would be easier to manage Bobby in the country.

On the way out of the shed, I notice wild sugar cane growing hard upon its walls – as high as my shoulder. I have to speak up. "Don't you think it is a little risky, Bob, having so much cane so close to your collection?" It is midsummer and the cane will soon die and the fires will come again.

Bob seems not to care. "Come back inside," he says. "I'll make us another cup of tea."

We go back inside. And talk resumes about science and history and politics, with nothing about family. I want answers. I have questions. Surely Bob is curious, but he isn't.

There is an interruption when Bob took Bobby back to his bedroom for his afternoon nap. Bobby takes some coaxing, but he can walk well enough, which is a surprise given his sitting posture.

Later on, Bobby begins to groan, so we go to see him. He is sitting up in bed, groaning and rocking, groaning and rocking, quite rhythmically.

"Here Bobby," I say. "Try the ukulele," and I hand him the ukulele I've brought. Bob had placed it beside the bed soon after I arrived. Bobby stops groaning and rocking. To my pleasure, he strums a few notes and, as he strums, I am able to get a good look at him. I can see some family traits: the shape of his nose, the heavy eyelids, a certain expression as he concentrates on his playing.

"He loves music," says Bob. "If I put on Mozart or Bach, he often quietens down and smiles. Sometimes he even laughs and claps his hands."

Late in his teens, Bob was on his way to being a concert violinist, according to my mother. Then he decided on the more practical career of dentistry. And he gave up playing the violin altogether because "he was a perfectionist".

"And that's why he's a great dentist," my mother added, "and that's why he had no more kids."

The day is wearing on. There is a beach restaurant booked for the evening a long way south, so I make my excuses and go in to say goodbye to Bobby. Putting a hand on his shoulder, I say, "See you later, mate."

Bobby, in return, stares at me blankly with his big brown eyes, with no sign of love or recognition.

"I've given him his meds," says Bob, who is standing right behind me. "Except I'll give him his insulin later. I don't want to finger-prick the poor fellow right now."

I say I understand, and we walk out to my car.

"Thanks for the ukulele," says Bob.

"Thanks for having me," I reply, and we shake hands and I get into my car and start the engine.

Before shifting into gear, I wind the window down and say, "I'll be back soon."

Bob waves and turns to go inside to attend to his son.

In my rear-view mirror, I watch the house recede, a house half consumed by tropical growth, a house set deep in the shadows of cedars and mango trees.

*

One day, maybe a year later, Bob calls to tell me that he is dying.

"Pancreas," Bob says. "It's everywhere, even in my head."

I tell him how sorry I am and ask him whether anything can be done.

"Nothing. Nothing can be done," he replies, "I'm just waiting for what comes next. I feel okay right now. They're giving me great drugs for the headaches. And my vision's still okay, so I can read."

I then say something feeble like "that's such bad luck". It's always hard to know what to say to people in these situations.

"I'm an expert on bad luck."

Bob's tone is matter-of-fact, flat.

I might have argued the toss, but we both know he is right.

We then go on to talk about the lady who has been lined up to permanently look after Bobby. The current carers are not up for it, according to Bob, and he does not want Bobby to go into a home. Bob tells me that he's made a big financial provision for Bobby's care. It might have explained the modest house.

I try to call Bob a month later, but there is just the burr-burring of a dead line. Work is busy. I plan to try again; and then, a few days later, I hear from a distant relative that Bob has died.

*

Driving north again, entering the latitude of sugar cane, I wonder whether I will drop in on Bobby. I am taking the back roads because they're pretty and because I'm vacillating about making the detour.

As I pass through endless rolling hills – pasture and forest, light and shade – Bobby's face slowly reassembles in my mind. It is a tragic face at first, latently handsome, but with a blankness of expression that betrays half-formed thoughts, the fault lines behind his wide, clear eyes; and then some Mozart comes on the radio and a broad smile forms on Bobby's face. His face becomes beatific. Bobby has become one of his own angels.

FIRELIGHT

SHE ASKS HIM WHY THE LAND BEYOND THE RIVER IS BURNED TO a crisp. It's no good asking him at the pub where he is always acting the fool and it's hard to get a straight answer to anything. So now she'll give him time and space to be serious. She's glad he's asked her along. It's probably the most romantic thing he's ever done. It's like a dream, watching him leaning back on outstretched arms, listening to him talk. She's sitting cross-legged, drawing patterns in the river sand with a bit of stick, saying nothing. God he can talk, she thinks. She's never realised there were so many words trapped inside. And he's stone cold sober.

*

This is Davo's story, more or less:

Last summer was as hot as hell. Me and Jimmie skipped work a few times to go swimming at the waterhole. Jim can barely swim and I have to watch him like a mother hen. Jim's been in trouble with the law lately. He gets on the grog and hits the missus. I've told him he's a fuckin' coward to hit a woman, but Jim just tells me to fuck off, says it's just the drink talking. He makes it up to her, but. Plays the good hubby for a while until the next big session. And so, when we go down to the waterhole, I don't take beer no more. Jim's me mate. I reckon he'll go to gaol for sure if it happens again. Jim's a bit simple if you ask me.

But why am I starting with Jimmie? You want to know what happened. Well, if it wasn't summer and wasn't fuckin' hot and if Jimmie had been around … well, then, maybe nuthin' would have happened.

I'm careful when it's hot. I don't use the chainsaw 'cause of sparks, and I put me butts out properly – which is hard to remember to do 'cause I normally throw'em out the car window or onto the ground. But you've got to set an example when yer in the volunteer bush fire brigade. My parole officer said it'd be good for me, and yeah, I reckon it's okay. The fire captain, Ray, he can be a pain in the arse – but we have a good laugh now and then and we've done some good things. My stepdad says I'm finally doing something useful which is great 'cause he generally calls me a useless bastard, 'specially after I do something really dumb like roll the tractor or shoot the neighbour's dog (I thought it was a fox). They wouldn't have me at first, the brigade, but I followed them to the fires and did odd jobs and brought cold beers and stuff. And I think they felt sorry for me after the blue at the pub.

About a year ago, I was playing the pub pokies, quietly minding me own business. Two girls, both not bad looking, especially the blonde, started playing on the next machine, the James Bond one. They spoke a language I didn't understand. I thought they were probably backpackers; we get a few. I guessed they spoke some English and I thought I might just chat them up a bit, but I'm not too good with women, as you can see. I usually need a lot of drink in me to talk to girls. Anyway, you wouldn't believe it; after just a couple of minutes their machine went berserk. They'd hit a jackpot. The only problem was, it turned out they were playing on a reserved machine. They should have looked, but then they were foreigners and you can't expect foreigners to know all the rules.

The machine was already in credit to the tune of thirty-five bucks. And worst of all, it was being used by a real prick called Ted Leary. Ted was over at the bar getting another drink, talking to June. Ted had the habit of pouring his entire dole down the pokies every Friday night, the silly bastard. And Mum says you can't beat the machines in the long run. "It's the law of averages," she says. She's clever, my mum.

I wasn't doing too well meself that evening and I have to tell you I was pretty jealous. But when I saw Ted coming at the girls, pissed as a newt, I got shit scared 'cause I knew I might have to get involved. There was no-one else around. Usually, I play the pokies with Jimmie, but Jimmie was away visiting his mum. Jimmie would have come in handy. Jimmie's built like a brick shit-house and I was worried 'cause Ted's a bloke with issues. Ted was a real bully at school. He'd sometimes hit people for no reason, no reason at all. Someone said he'd gone mental 'cause his father used to beat him up.

Anyway, the girls didn't see Ted coming and I stayed put at first, pretending not to notice what was going on. But it started off about as badly as I expected.

"You fuckin' bitches," said Ted.

They looked up, really surprised. Then they looked at each other and said some foreign words, and I could tell they didn't know what to do.

"You fuckin' bitches."

Ted was leaning right over them with one hand on their machine and the other on the back of one of their chairs. None of us could understand what they were saying. They were German, I found out later, from Germany.

"It's my fuckin' machine."

One of them said something like "What?"

"My fuckin' machine. What are youse? Fuckin' German bitches? Fuckin' fascists. Now piss off. Get out of my pub."

The girls backed away.

"Go back to your fuckin' country – or do you want one out the back right now – find out what a real man is? I'll bet your men are limp-dicked bastards. Where are your blokes, anyway?"

This was too much. I put down me schooner, got off the stool and squared up to Ted – trying not to look scared although I was practically pissing in me pants. Ted's eyes were bulging. His face was red. He was like a big, mad dog let off its chain. And Jesus, he stank. You could smell the booze and BO from a mile away.

I knew Ted had bikie mates. They were into selling drugs and they had a record of doin' some serious damage to people who got in their way. There was a story that our local cop, Bill Lee, got up one morning to find the whole crew making him breakfast in his own house. "Thought we'd make you a lovely breakfast, Bill," they said, and that was just to show who was boss.

Anyway, I said to Ted, "No, you piss off, Ted, you fuckin' loser – pickin' on girls – fuckin' coward." I couldn't believe what I was saying. To tell you the truth, I would never have guessed I had the balls.

The sheilas were watching from a corner of the room. At least I was looking good in front of them.

"Turd face," said Ted. "You're a pathetic piece of shit. Get out of me sight before I rearrange your face, you dick-brain."

But I stood me ground.

I could see Ted wanted me to hit him first. That's 'cause it's much easier with the magistrate if you don't make the first move.

"Your sister's gonna get one from me. She's an ugly bitch."

And of course I fell for it – dumb bastard that I am.

I took a swing but was surprised at how easily Ted dodged it, given how big he is. Then came the nasty shock. Ted pulled a skinning knife from his back pocket, and I wasn't quick enough. He slashed me across the arm and might have done worse if June hadn't got between us. God, I love June. You know June? She does Fridays at the bar.

"Back off, Ted," June said. "Piss off. You fuckin' lunatic."

And Ted backed off. There was no way he was going to hurt June. I reckon he was soft on her.

And you should have seen the blood. Blood everywhere. I had to go to the doctor and get stitches. But it all worked out well in the end. Ted got six months and I got … I got on well with one of the girls. Not the blonde one, though. The other one. Goes to show, doing the right thing does pay. And people were impressed. Davo's got balls, I heard them say, and I joined the brigade soon afterwards.

Fighting fires is a lot more fun than packing at the supermarket. Sure, there's a lot of muckin' around and boring training exercises and hazard reduction – but when a real fire comes, let me tell you, it's full on. You know when the boss is worried 'cause he gets really cranky, which says something 'cause he's a cranky bastard most of the time anyway. And there's something else. If Ray's on the radio and starts taking his glasses on and off and wiping them all the time, you know it's a big deal. It's compulsive or something like that, according to Mum. Anyway, Ray barks orders and we hop to it. When there's a fire, Ray's the king and we don't give him no backchat. A whole crew lost their lives somewhere a few years ago and it turns out that some of the blokes, God rest their souls, weren't good listeners.

After the fires last summer, the Governor came. She gave a long speech I couldn't follow, except the bit at the end: that we were heroes. And I reckon it was true. People we didn't know bought us drinks at the Royal. Ma said I was a good boy. My stepdad said I done him proud. And I got to say that it made me feel real good. For just a little while I wasn't a shit-kicker. Not many people are tough enough to stand the heat for hours and hours. Not many people risk their lives fighting fires. Last summer we rescued a little girl's pony. She gave me a hug and I'll never forget it.

I've always liked fires. We used to light some big ones in the backyard on the June long weekend. But you gotta be careful. One time a hot coal went down me gumboot and jammed up against me ankle. Jesus it hurt. I'll never forget the pain. And I've still got the scar.

I like the way fires start from little and then grow and grow. I like to watch the flames leap about and render everything down. And there's the smell of burning eucalypt; most people like this, but I also love the other smells, of sulphur and wet ash and melting plastic. Fires are wild. They're free. They take no shit from anyone, except us, of course.

This season was turning out to be depressing, remember? No fires but tinder dry, something to do with El Nino. That's a weather pattern, according to Ray. Apart from the rain in autumn, nuthin', a never-ending drought, country as dry as a dead dingo's donger. I watched the news with my stepdad a few days ago and there was more stuff about global warming. My stepdad has had family in the district for practically forever. He says that global warming is an idea coming from city wankers who have no idea about the bush, about nature. It's been this dry before, he says. And I agree with him, of course. I know what's good for me. But I do wonder. You look down from the riverbank and there are just separate little puddles where once a paddle steamer used to go. But some good comes out of it. It's easy to catch fish and collect clams. Everything's rounded up into just a few little bits of water. And the pig shootin's really good 'cause the pigs crowd up near the river, as the smaller streams are all gone and the dams are mainly empty.

Ray had been saying for weeks that the fire risk was extreme and that we should all be available. Which is easy for me. I'm always around and they'll always let me off work if there's a big fire. "It's the least we can do," says Mrs Heron, the store manager, the old witch. Everyone's nervous here 'cause of the national park coming up hard on the town from two sides. There's a lot of growth 'cause the Aborigines don't burn off anymore like in the olden days. And I don't mind bein' on call 'cause fighting fires is much more fun than packing shelves.

So I was waiting and waiting. You can go mad waiting for a friggin' fire that doesn't come. Jimmie usually keeps me company even though he's not allowed near a fire. The school hall burned down a few years ago and people think it was him. But I know it wasn't him. What would he have got outta that? And Jimmie's me mate. You've gotta stick by your mates.

But I have to say I was getting pretty bored. There's only so much drinkin' and shootin' and pokie playin' a man can do. And I was sick of DVDs and computer games as well. And that's why I went out into the Pingilla shrub Friday arvo on me own – I was bored shitless and I'd also had enough of Jimmie. Jimmie never lets up about the same things: AFL and cricket. Jimmie needs to get out more, broaden his conversation.

So I loaded the ute up with a few tinnies and took me Winchester .44/40 lever action just in case there was something to shoot. The dog went on the tray with the diesel and the spare tyre. I love me ute. It's got alloy mag wheels and red paint and a turbocharger.

The Pingilla shrub is a fire hazard according to Ray: 30,000 hectares of bonfire fuel, he says. And let me tell you, it wasn't easy getting in. It was stinkin' hot. Everything was clapped out, but the bush was still thick. Branches kept brushin' the side of the ute, making noise like ladies' fingernails. I was worried I'd scratch the duco and I thought of going back. Fuckin' council can't even keep the main tracks clear. They're fuckin' hopeless.

When I was about seven k's in, which means I was near the top of the big hill over there, I caught a glimpse of some white duco on a sidetrack. I thought I'd take a look and so I stopped and walked towards it. A white commodore came into view, and would you believe it, there was Ted, crouched down beside some bushes. He didn't hear me 'cause the cicadas were so loud – you could go deaf from the cicadas. At first I thought he was having a bog, but then I saw that he was lightin' leaves with a cigarette lighter, the daft bastard. I couldn't think why he'd be doin' that. I'd heard of fires for insurance or maybe there was a drug bust coming and a fire would be a distraction or get rid of evidence or something. Or maybe Ted had completely flipped. Anyway, I watched and watched. A small wisp of smoke rose up at first and then a lot more and then I could see some flames. Ted got back into his car – but, you wouldn't credit it, the car wouldn't start. You shoulda seen his face. It was a study, I can tell you. I heard the engine turning over, so I don't think it was a flat battery.

Well, I had to make a decision pretty quick. Give Ted a lift or leave him trapped? There wasn't much time to think. So what do you reckon I did? That's right, I left him! One thing me dad taught me, before he buggered off, was that some people just can't be changed. If I'd have saved Ted he'd probably be at it again next year or the year after. So I did all of us a favour, I backed off and got into me ute. As I hooned off down the track I could just make out Ted running after me. By crikey he was moving. I'm not a religious man, but I said my paternosters on the way back.

By the time I got home you could see smoke in the distance. So I made a cup of tea and ate a sandwich while I waited for the call to come. And it did.

"Big Fire in the Pingilla," said Ray, not a man of many words.

It sure was. It was the biggest fire ever. Ray just couldn't stop fiddling with his glasses as we drove in, all of us sweating away in full kit. The fire nearly took the town, but we saved it after three days of ball-breaking work. We were heroes again.

On the night we stood down, a hollow tree strangely lit up on the big hill. It wasn't far from where I last saw Ted. It burned like a beacon all night. You could see it for miles and miles. We didn't bother to go and put it out, though. It was the only thing left. The Gamilaraay people in town just shook their heads. Never happened in their day. Not like this.

And I never told no-one except you about Ted. I guess it's you and the firelight over the river and the stars that got me started. 'Cause you're a lovely girl. If we're gonna be an item, I want you to know everything, including this: that I don't take no shit from no-one.

THREE SOMERSAULTS

—

"DON'T BE NERVOUS, THEY'RE GOING TO LOVE YOU."

They are at the stern of the ferry, leaning over the gunwale, watching the water welling up from the propeller like molasses. In the white wake, seabirds swoop and dive. The coast has receded to nothing, so that, now, almost everything is blue. The sea, ultramarine with a touch of phthalo green, has merged with an empty, cloudless sky. You might say the day is perfect.

I cannot see their faces, but I guess they are in their thirties. Their hands are resting on the wet railing, his left hand brushing her right. They are leaning in to one another.

The man is tall, powerfully built, with blond hair done up in a man-bun. The woman is petite, a full foot shorter, with mid-length brown hair. Both of them are wearing stylish jackets, the ones that come down mid-thigh, sixties style. Possibly, they are beautiful.

I would like to hear more of what they are saying, but their words are lost in the sound of churning sea, the shriek of gulls, the chatter of passengers. In lieu of words, in the idleness of a lazy summer day, in a waking sleep, I give the couple form, make them real. In short, a fiction is invented – only, is it fiction? In the course of space and time, all things will come to pass.

*

125

"Don't be nervous, they're going to love you."

The young woman is talking to her man.

"Really, I mean it; don't be nervous, Aaron. They'll be pleased I've found someone. They might seem a bit uptight, but they're not really. We had hard times when I was growing up, when Dad was trying to get his practice going. They do carry on a bit, but they're lovely, really, once you get to know them."

"Do you think your mother will like the scarf?"

They had bought the scarf before they left Melbourne.

"She'll love it."

"Your Dad, though, he's not going to want to talk about Brexit or Trump or China, is he? If we get into politics, he'll think I'm an idiot."

"You worry too much, Aaron. Dad doesn't talk politics unless he's had a few drinks. He'll just do banter until he gets to know you. You can do banter, can't you, baby?"

"Anyway," he says, ignoring the question, "you look great. They'll be excited to see *you*."

"That's the thing; the focus will be on me to start with. So don't worry, my darling!" She presses in further against him while he stares out over the sea.

"Things might change, though, when we start talking about the future. Leave that bit to me, will you?"

Aaron doesn't respond. His mind has drifted. He is thinking about diving – in particular, the execution of an inward with three somersaults and half twist.

*

Amelia's father picks them up at the wharf. On the short drive to the house, he says little beyond the usual pleasantries: weather, flight, the day's plans.

The house, Georgian, modestly grand, sits on a small hill, facing the English coast. Tiny birds flit in and out of the blossoming hawthorn as they come up the drive. The family must have heard the car approaching because they are out on the gravel when Aaron and Amelia pull up. First comes a large dog, scratching at the duco, all wet nose and drool and wagging tail. Amelia's mother follows, grabbing the dog by the collar, saying, "Off, Ralph, off, bad dog, bad!" She is wearing a cardigan and pearls and a Barbour jacket, looking like someone straight out of *Country Life*. She hugs Amelia and steps back to appraise her daughter.

"Darling, you look marvellous, simply marvellous. Look at that tan!" And then, "And this must be Aaron! Even more handsome in real life. So nice of you to come straight out here, after such a long trip."

Amelia's mother is small, like her daughter. She also has the same sparkling, searching eyes, the same delicacy of bone structure and, apparently, the same force of personality.

Aaron puts on the smile he usually reserves for new members at the gym. He tries to say something, but Amelia's mother continues to talk at speed. "Do come in! We've got John's old room ready."

Aaron has been briefed never, ever, to ask about John. He died in an accident, in India, many years ago. According to Amelia it's a "no-go" subject; it's how her family handles disaster, she says: "We just don't talk about it."

Richard, Amelia's younger brother, is next. He bowls up to Aaron and shakes his hand vigorously. "Christ, another Aussie!" he says, holding Aaron in his eyes for a moment or two longer than is polite.

Finally, Amelia's paternal grandfather hobbles towards them. "Pleased to meet you, Aaron," he says. "We've heard so much about you. First the legend, now the man!" There is only the barest hint of a smile.

*

The drawing room overlooks a field where brown-and-white cows are grazing. All else is sea and sky. A fire burns in the hearth despite the warmth of the day.

"Coffee, tea?" asks Amelia's mother.

"Coffee, tea?" echoes her father in disdain. "Nearly midday. Sun's over the yardarm somewhere. Let's have a drink, shall we? Cause for celebration, isn't it? Our beautiful girl back from Oz with her man. What would you like, Aaron? I know what you'll have, Amelia: a G and T. And you, Dickie, my boy … I can still smell the booze from last night. Hair of the dog, eh?"

"Don't let my husband bully you, Aaron. You can just have tea or coffee if you like," says Amelia's mother, in what seems to be a practised interjection.

"Well, if everyone's having a drink, I'll have a vodka and tonic, if that's okay."

"Sorry, don't keep vodka. Hate the stuff myself." Amelia's father is already on his way to the drinks cabinet.

"Beer, then?"

"Beer it is. Only got full strength, though, sorry; can't see the point of the light beer."

"That's fine, Mr Aldercott."

"Frank, please. No need for formality. Not here."

"How was the flight?" asks Richard to fill the ensuing silence "I've only ever flown as far as Majorca. Must be bloody long!"

It is Amelia who answers. Perhaps she's worried he'll say something banal or embarrassing – or perhaps it's in her nature.

Amelia is quick, fast off the block, as her mother seems to be. *I'm too sensitive*, he thinks. *A champion must rise above the doubts.*

When he did poorly in his leaving certificate, Aaron's father told him that he was not a smart man. His father, a real estate agent, said that *he* had learned to calibrate his expectations. Aaron, in turn, had learned that life is not all about a university degree. It is about luck and hard work and drive. There is academic memory. There is muscle memory. He is gifted with the latter, so he has recently been spending most of his free time trying to qualify for the Australian springboard diving team.

"Well, you know, bloody long," says Amelia. "We thought about premium economy, but the prices were insane. Poor Aaron had his knees up under his chin. They should reserve the aisle seats for tall people. That's what I think."

Amelia has been earning a good income as a stylist for the fashion industry. This is how they met – when Aaron was moonlighting as a model to get a bit of cash together for travel and, maybe, one day, a house. And now this – plans for babies. Permanence.

Amelia is in her late thirties. Aaron is twenty-nine. Amelia never lets Aaron forget that her "clock" is ticking. A pretty face is a trap, she says. It makes a person feel ageless, invincible. Retired models have told her so.

They are seated around a large coffee table, Aaron next to Amelia on one sofa, the rest of the family on the other, facing them like an interviewing committee.

"First time in England, Aaron?" Richard asks.

"Actually, first time out of Australia."

"Well, what do you think so far?"

"Very nice. Very green. I've never seen such deep greens."

*

After lunch, they go back to the drawing room for coffee. Through the big French windows, it is apparent that the weather has changed. Clouds have gathered. Light rain is falling across a flat, grey sea. No boats are visible, but the flap of luffing sails carries in the breeze. Four bottles of red wine have been downed and everyone is drowsy, struggling to maintain the flow of conversation.

"We hear you're in the fitness industry; is that right?" Amelia's father asks.

Amelia answers. "Aaron manages a gym in the centre of Melbourne, Dad, a really nice club. He trains Members of State Parliament and lawyers. All sorts of people. Aaron's also a champion diver. Remember the photos I sent from the state trials?"

"That's marvellous. *You* could use a bit of gym, couldn't you, Frank?" says Amelia's mother.

"Golf's enough for me. Play golf, Aaron?"

"Sorry, I don't. I play a bit of soccer, sometimes. The diving keeps me pretty busy."

"Frank's very big on the nineteenth hole, aren't you, Frank?"

"Sorry?" asks Aaron.

"You know, the club bar!"

"Oh, I see." And then another silence and more intermittent conversation like desultory gunfire after a battle. The old man in the club chair is keeping his own counsel, sometimes nodding off, sometimes rousing himself with a start.

When the grandfather clock in the hallway chimes three, he suddenly perks up. "Tell us about your family, Aaron. Not convicts, are they?"

There is a little titter from the others at the odd change in topic.

"Really, Albert? Old line, that one!" says Amelia's mother.

"You need new material, Grandpa," says Richard.

Undeterred, the old man maintains his line of questioning; his smile is gone, his eyes are intensely focused on Aaron. "I'm guessing Anglo–Irish with a bit of something – let me guess, French blood?"

"Actually, my father was Norwegian, my mother was Armenian."

"How marvellous! How exotic!" exclaims Amelia's mother. "We are so boring. Just generations of the same thing. And look at Dickie here, pinnacle of a thousand years of breeding, aren't you, Dickie?"

"Whatever, Mum." Dickie has recently dropped out of university and is living in the caretaker's cottage.

"Dickie's learning sail-making, aren't you, Dickie? Who wants to be a boring lawyer at Temple like Daddy, in any case?" says Amelia.

"Always wanted to go to Australia, you know," Amelia's father continues. "Never found the time. Such a long way. Hear there are some great golf courses."

"I wouldn't know," Aaron replies.

"If you come out, Aaron will take you go-kart racing, won't you, Aaron? You forgot to mention the go-kart racing. He's taken me. Really great fun. Terrifying, though. You're so close to the ground." Amelia's relaxed pose – she is leaning back on the couch, an arm across the top of a large cushion – is at odds with the speed of her words.

"Really, is that so?" replies Amelia's father. The coffee is finished. He is waving an empty whisky tumbler in the air. "Another drink, anyone? Aaron? Amelia?" There is a slight slur in his voice. He is looking flushed. Aaron can see capillaries spreading Gorgon-like across his face. Glasses are refilled, and the afternoon wears on.

*

"But your people? Who are your people?" Amelia's grandfather returns to life, maybe half an hour later.

"He's told you, Grandpa," Amelia answers.

"Well, what are you going to do after the gym? Just a phase, isn't it, dear boy?"

"Actually, I like it. I have two junior trainers under me."

"Well done you," says Richard.

"My people were miners," says Amelia's grandfather. "We were poor as church mice. Had to go to night school, you know, when I wasn't at the coalface. Bloody hard work, you know."

"The coalface, Grandpa?" asks Amelia.

"No, night school. And the second job as a bookkeeper to support Frank at university. And Frank's done well, haven't you, Frank?"

Amelia's father, who hasn't spoken for a few minutes, suddenly pipes up, "Don't you think it's better to live over here, Amelia? Fashion industry's so much bigger over here, isn't that so, Bunny?" He only calls his wife Bunny when he is getting drunk. Amelia had warned Aaron, "If he starts calling Mum 'Bunny', watch out!"

"That's what we were going to talk about, Dad. Aaron and I are going to settle down in Melbourne. Have babies. That's what I was going to tell you. Aaron has proposed, and I've said yes. We're going to get a ring from Hancock's on the way back. I told Aaron, 'Mummy and Daddy will like it traditional.' It's the least we can do. Sorry, Daddy, if it wasn't such a rushed trip, I would have got Aaron to speak to you first."

"The least you can do," echoes her grandfather from the club chair.

"Really, Grandpa! What does that mean?" Amelia shoots back.

"Yes, Albert, do leave them alone," says Amelia's mother. "They're grown-ups. They can do as they please. We're delighted, Aaron, we really are." There is a lowering of eyes that says otherwise.

"We've come a long way," murmurs Amelia's grandfather as his head dips and he nods off again, back into a postprandial stupor.

Amelia's father moves the conversation to sport. Everyone is interested to know what Aaron thinks about performance-enhancing drugs and ball-tampering and other tricks of the trade.

When this subject is exhausted, the old man suddenly rouses himself again. "Gym trainer, eh? Pays good money, does it? How can you raise a family, working in a gym?"

"For God's sake, Albert, Aaron's a manager. He doesn't just show people how to lift weights."

"Long way we've come," repeats the old man.

"You mean our family?" asks Richard.

"Yes, long way."

"Sorry, Aaron," Richard says. "Grandpa always gets a bit tetchy in the afternoons."

As they talk on, occasional words flutter up from the old man like game birds on the fen. "Gym trainer. From Australia!"

The old man fumbles for his walking stick and, with enormous trembling effort, levers himself upright using a side-table for support.

"I've just remembered," he says. "I've forgotten to post something." He turns and leaves the room.

There is the sound of the front door slamming shut, followed by the slow shuffle of old man's shoes on gravel. It is Sunday. There is no post on Sunday.

*

They call the engagement off three weeks later, on the last night in London, where they are staying at a nice hotel in Bloomsbury. After dinner, they have an argument over something minor, and things escalate.

Amelia says she needs a shower, apparently calming down – and then, suddenly, she is back in the room, hair everywhere, face wet with tears, saying, "You don't get things, do you, Aaron? You live on another bloody planet. You know when Grandpa walked out? You know what the problem was? The problem wasn't that you were insulted. The problem was that you weren't. You didn't even get it."

*

And now this: Melbourne; no Amelia; the flight home a cramped misery not improved by alcohol; a taxi to the door, in darkness, on almost empty streets.

He tries to sleep but can't. When the green digits of the bedside clock hit four am, he gives up and gets dressed and drives to the Olympic pool.

*

In the aquatic centre, in the hour before daybreak, a naked man is floating in the air, illuminated in the faint light of salt-washed windows. He might be an angel, or a saint in a basilica. You watch him lift his arms out wide. You watch a faint crucifix appear on the far wall. Otherwise, everything is darkness, everything is still.

*

Aaron has forgotten his towel, his swimmers, his goggles. He could not find the master switch for the lights – although lighting is unnecessary. Diving is "cerebral", as his coach puts it. You shut out external stimuli and begin with the notion of a body moving in space with reference to nothing but time. Then you add self-awareness, the trim of arms, the flexion of legs. And then memory – everything to be recalled – the movement, the rhythm, the voyage through microseconds.

He closes his eyes and visualises the dive, happy in the knowledge that once his feet slip through tiny rings of water, he will be briefly free. Before the surfacing. The sucking in of air. The noise.

*

I watch him lower his arms to his side, flex his knees, shift his gravity slightly forward.

And then voices from below, followed by a stunning explosion of light. Aaron straightens himself and takes a step backwards on the trembling board.

Below him is an empty pool – no water, just wheelbarrows and bags of cement and crossed tape.

It is at this moment his true journey begins – this moment when he knows he is a lucky man.

*

And now the ferry docks. The tall man is shouldering his carryall and putting an arm around the brown-haired woman as they step back into the crowd. I stir myself and gather up my bags of mainland shopping and make my way to the gangplank. My cottage, my easel, await. I am the last to disembark.

DOLPHIN BOY

WHEN DOLPHIN BOY VANISHED IN THE SUMMER SEA, A MOTHER lost a son and I lost a friend. They were sorry at the school, too. They said so in letters and on TV.

Bon voyage, Dolphin Boy, *bon voyage. Adieu, mon ami!*

I remember saying these words as I scrambled over headland rocks trying to follow the progress of the pod. Why French? I wonder now. I suppose it was because my heart was bursting. I didn't say much else, because I was trying to catch my breath. I wasn't too fit, even back then.

When I got to the beach that day, my cotton shirt was clinging to my back. The southerly hadn't come, and it was unbearably humid. The water near the shoreline was glazed smooth and green. Everything was still. The clouds above me were still. The Norfolk Island pines were still. Everything was freeze-framed. Yet out towards the horizon, you could see the clouds scudding southwards. The distant ocean was turning a brilliant blue. The tension between sea and sky was resolving. Perhaps this is what drew Dolphin Boy and his friends away: better places, better times, things unfelt by us, things unseen. We'll never know.

The beach is just a short walk down the road from our old house. It has headlands at each end like clasps on a necklace.

It's a good surfing beach. I like to body surf as long as there are no dumpers. I know someone who was paralysed from the waist down by a dumper. In any case, there were no dumpers because the humid air had ironed everything out.

I never go straight in. It's wise to check for sharks and undercurrents and, back in those days, I was always on the lookout for Dolphin Boy and the pod. They didn't stay between the flags. They did whatever they liked, and this filled me with envy. I'd watch them come close in and catch waves. They'd roll upside down and blow streams of bubbles. I could tell they were singing, although I never heard their song.

At first, there was no sign of the dolphins or Dolphin Boy, and then a swell came up and suddenly there they were, suspended like microbes on a slide, half-a-dozen or more black darts shooting across the face of a wave, and Dolphin Boy, blue-finned and orange-goggled, following behind.

Dolphin Boy was actually more man than boy by this time; in some ways, more fish than man. His pectoral muscles were huge. His black curly hair had bleached into one great orange tousle. His skin had thickened and acquired an even darker hue. His rubber fins were the last thing you'd see on a dive. He'd clap them in the air as he disappeared under the surface, and you wouldn't see him again for several minutes, which made the lifeguards nervous. Back on land he'd sometimes make a little dolphin cry, a sort of "arf, arf", and toss his head back in little jerks.

Generally, the pod and Dolphin Boy liked to work the break. They liked to follow the curve of coast, fifty or a hundred metres offshore. But while I was drying off that day, in that pretty vacant state of mind that comes with drying off, I felt uneasy. I looked around, and at first everything seemed totally in order. And then I spotted the pod heading out to sea with Dolphin Boy following, freestyling for all he was worth, five strokes to a breath. I had been growing increasingly worried that Dolphin Boy was losing his sense of limitation. And now I had the proof. So I threw down my towel and ran to the small southern headland, following the faster shoreline route, as it was low tide. It was hard going, but I was wearing my best flip-flops. You can go through a lot of flip-flops on coastal rocks when it's hot and the rubber is soft. Even so, by the time I got there, my knees were grazed and I had cut a finger on an oyster's shell. The blood was attracting flies. *Jesus*, I remember thinking, *how do flies get all the way out here?* But they do, I tell you.

I climbed the little pyramid of rocks on the point and saw that Dolphin Boy was already a long way off. I could just make out his bobbing head in the deep, dark, rolling swell. Even further out was the pod. They were hard to pick, but every now and then I caught a glimpse of a fin or arching back. I noticed that one of them, perhaps an adolescent, had gone back to check on Dolphin Boy. It circled him several times before diving and then breaching. For a brief moment it was suspended in mid-air, a small black comma in the blue sky. Then it landed sideways, making a decent splash, as if to say to me, "It's okay, man, it's okay, we'll look after your boy. Don't worry!" But I was very sad. Somehow, I knew they weren't coming back.

When I returned to the beach, the sun was setting. Dolphin Boy's mother was there, standing on the shoreline, staring out to sea. Her face was stone. She didn't move from the spot until after dark when the moon came out and a line of glistening ocean stretched eastwards, showing the way.

Over the years that followed I dreamed of where they might be. They were beautiful dreams of tropical islands and pretty fish. They made me think about the wide mystery of our planet.

*

Dolphin Boy had appeared in our lives in the usual manner: a perky, roly-poly baby brought home from hospital one winter morning, all milky and wide-eyed. He lived with his mother in a flat next to our house.

In no time, Dolphin Boy was toddling beside a new pram-bound sister and patting our dog at the front gate, asking lots of questions. He was an intelligent child. We said this to his mother when we met her on the street, usually on Monday evenings when the wheelie bins went out. She wasn't particularly sociable. Her private life was a source of mystery.

Dolphin Boy's real name was Kale. I am proud to say that I was the one who gave him the name "Dolphin Boy". When we let Kale's mother teach him to swim in our pool, we were amazed at how he pushed away from her immediately and set out swimming without any lessons. The name just came naturally.

Kale's mother took him and his sister, Oleana, down to the beach every weekend. His sister did the normal small-child things. Kale, on the other hand, spent all his time in the water. While Oleana made sandcastles, Kale swam about on his own, happy as Larry. In fact, he'd never want to get out of the water.

One day she was really struggling to get him to cooperate, and a lightning storm was coming. "Come on, Kale," she said. "You can watch TV if you get out now."

Kale was lying in the shallows, stretched out, fully submerged except for his head.

"No, Mummy," he said. "I like it here."

He must have been about eight. I saw his mother take a few steps forward so that she was knee-deep in water. I watched the hem of her dress grow dark and wet. She grabbed Kale's arm, but he struggled and broke free.

"Look at you, Kale, your skin's all wrinkled. We've got to go home. There's a big storm coming and Oleana needs to be fed."

Kale backed away in silence. He slid into the deeper water, ignoring his mother's pleas. I can still see his large blue swimming fins and his goggles with long redundant bits of rubber strap. I still remember his black Speedos. He had a typical eight-year-old's body, with not a gram of fat and not a single strand of body hair. While all gangly and pigeon-toed on land, he was all muscle and sinew in the water. In the water, his dark limbs worked in beautiful unison.

In desperation, his mother went in until she was waist deep and getting drenched in the shore break, waiting for an opportunity that never seemed to come. At the same time, she was trying to keep an eye on Oleana.

I was close by, so I took off my shirt and put my wallet and watch in my upturned Panama hat and waded in after her. "Hi, Teuila," I said. "Want a hand?"

"Thanks, Ed. He's difficult when he wants to be."

I dived in and had him out of the water in no time. We joked. And this is how we became friends.

As Dolphin Boy grew, bribes were needed. Eventually, he wouldn't come out, no matter what anyone did. He was growing more resistant to the cold. He was wrinkling up less. His lungs were growing stronger. He could stay underwater for a full four minutes. I timed it. All up, he just didn't seem to need spells on land like he used to.

Dolphin Boy agreed to go to school on the condition that he was hosed down at lunchtime. This was onerous for the staff, but they humoured him because he excelled at basketball. The school team was on a roll. Kale was able to get the ball in the hoop from the other end of the court, no problem.

"American basketball league for sure – if he grows tall enough." Dolphin Boy's ecstatic coach said these words after a big win. I was there. I was often there, standing in for his mother who had taken on a Royal Commission. She was apparently a lawyer of some renown.

But the going wasn't easy. Kale spent increasing amounts of time in the principal's office, or otherwise engaged with psychologists and counsellors.

"Isn't it lonely – not being with the other kids?" I asked him one morning when he was about eleven and waiting for the school bus.

Kale just stared at me in that contemptuous way that kids do when asked about something they feel is self-evident. I remember noticing that his freckles were fading.

And then he said, "I do have friends, Mr Nome. Dolphins are my friends. Dolphins know everything, like where that crashed plane is and why the Bermuda Triangle is there. And they're funny. And they can do what they like."

"Do you have any friends at school?" I asked. I was concerned for him. He was my little mate. I watched him drop his eyes and make little fists by his side. You could see the muscles in his hands tightening and relaxing, clenching and unclenching. It's a sure sign of tension. It's in the book I bought on body language. You need to understand that if you're going to be any good at poker. It's how we ended up with a nice house near the beach.

"Not really, Mr Nome, but they're not as mean as they were. Not after Mrs Zhu told everyone at assembly to be nice to me or else. And everyone's afraid of Mrs Zhu. Someone saw her kill a cat just by looking at it. And everyone's happy when I score a goal at basketball or win a swimming race. So I don't get things like the sardine treatment anymore."

He went on to tell me how he'd been force-fed sardines by a group of boys led by a monstrous child called Dwayne. He pointed Dwayne out to me one day at the school gate. Dwayne was built like a brick shit-house, even though he was only eleven years old.

*

When Dolphin Boy wasn't at the beach, he was usually in our backyard pool, which gave me the opportunity to try and win him over on the value of education.

While he bobbed about in my nicely filtered water, I'd sit on the edge trying to get him to see reason. I should have packed him off to school but, truth be told, I didn't mind the company.

"Come on, Kale," I'd say. "You've got to do your schoolwork, mate. I know you love the sea, but you've got to earn a buck eventually. If you study hard you could become a marine biologist or an oceanographer. You could join the navy. You could even look after dolphins at the zoo!"

The latter suggestion earned a scornful look and a lecture about the wickedness of impounding God's creatures.

I persisted, though. Even when he breached and dived into the chlorine depths in a show of adolescent defiance, I'd continue to make my case. Over the years, I've learned the value of patience. I don't think my entreaties worked, but I was rewarded with tales of underwater gardens and lost cities and giant manta rays. Kale was particularly fond of telling me about the enchanted pink dolphins of the Amazon. When the moon is full and twinkling on the river mouth, these dolphins transform themselves into humans so they can visit the misty, stilted villages. For Dolphin Boy, this might have been Utopia.

Often in the long, lonely evenings, I'd also just sit by the pool and listen. I think it was appreciated. Everyone else never let up with the lectures. And over time, Kale showed some improvement. He started getting better grades, and the school fitted out a small dolphin pool at the back of his classroom, a converted Jacuzzi. Things were looking up.

"We must be adaptive," said Mrs Zhu on Speech Day. "I'm proud to say that here at Headland High, we don't take a one-size-fits-all approach." Kale was getting a "Most Improved" prize, and I was sitting next to his mother. We'd been late. Everyone had stared at us as we squeezed our way through the tight rows of folding chairs. It had been a job getting Kale out of the bathtub in Teuila's van and into the marquee.

It was a joy seeing Kale up on the dais, all smiles, very pleased with himself, dressed normally: no goggles, no flippers, no Speedos. Thank God.

*

That was a very long time ago. Years later, dolphins came back into my life. I was at Pacific World, waiting for the eleven o'clock dolphin show, eating a dripping ice-cream, sitting on a forum of benches surrounding a large empty pool. People treat you like a fool when you're very old. There are no more play subscriptions or museum talks or challenging books for old bastards like me; you just get taken to spectacles like dolphin shows and garden festivals. They think I'm losing my marbles, going the same way as poor old Shirley, but they're wrong; I'm still as sharp as a tack.

It was turning out to be a pretty average dolphin show. I've seen a few over the years. But when one of the dolphins came over to our side of the pool, I was stunned. It was Dolphin Boy, without a doubt.

"What a beautiful big dolphin you've become," I said, although he couldn't hear me. "But you didn't get away, after all. We never truly escape, do we, any of us? And look at your friends! I'm sorry to see that everyone has been captured. How did they get you? Where did you go? It's been twenty years, for God's sake."

I had so many questions. But then a voice piped up from the row behind. "Come now, Ed, please sit down."

I realised that in the emotion of the moment I had stood straight up from my wheelchair. I didn't even think that I could stand anymore. Of course, I sat straight back down again, marvelling at my newfound mobility. I didn't want to block people's view. I just sat and watched the rest of the show with tears rolling down my cheeks.

And then the voice behind me said, "Time to go now, Ed, it's a long drive."

"No, I'll wait for my wife," I said.

"Your wife died a long time ago, sweetie, I'm sorry."

It was one of the nicer carers. Her family was in Asia somewhere. She often told me about them and their lives on the delta and I thought she'd understand.

"We live together near the beach," I insisted.

"What beach, Ed? There's no beach within a hundred miles of where we live."

"Well, I want to go home, to my old house."

"You don't live there anymore, Ed. You live with us. In our home, the special home. The bus is waiting."

Normally, I do what I'm told. I've always done what I'm told.

But this time, they had to pull me away.

Suddenly, all I wanted to do was to go down to the pool.

And hug Dolphin Boy.

And ask him about the sea.

ARCADIA

NIGHT WAS OUR TIME. HALF SHADOWED, FACING EACH OTHER, the two of us would talk for hours. The light was soft and indirect, you understand – street light; stairwell light; on occasion, moonlight. With the sliding doors shut, we were, in a sense, entombed.

We'd talk while roaches scuttled on the floor and spiders as big as dinner plates slipped under heavy doors. The spiders were always looking for a feed. Reassuringly, they had no appetite for anything bigger than a roach. We liked the spiders – so dainty they were, so fleet of foot, so precise. We never liked to see them hurt.

This was the backdrop to our "deep and meaningful" chats: an empty space, a confluence of corridors and sliding doors. The latter were like lungs. Opening, closing. Fresh air coming in and out like breath. When they stopped the doors at night, after the people had gone, there was a sense of suffocation.

When I say "deep and meaningful", I do mean *deep* and I do mean *meaningful*. Tasha never liked small talk. She liked to analyse. For example, she told me not so long ago that I should have greater self-esteem. She said that the people in my life don't value me enough. And then she asked me whether I was happy.

"Happy? You mean now?" I asked her, disingenuously, in the sepulchral tone I reserve for late at night.

"No, silly; I mean cosmically. Are you happy in a cosmic sense?"

I said, "Sort of."

She said, "Why's that?"

I said, "I'm not quite sure – my life's vaguely frustrating."

When she asked me why, I had no satisfactory answer.

How would I describe Tasha? Sweet, I guess, empathetic, possibly a little too intrusive. There have been occasions when I've had to ask her to back off.

"What about leaving a bit of mystery in the mix?" I said to her recently, when she was probing aspects of my early years – things I'd rather not talk about.

There was always a melancholic air about Tasha. Possibly, it was a source of attraction: two sad souls teaming up – only, in my book, two negatives don't make a positive. Still, there has always been a certain electricity between us. When we're together, a thousand volts run through me – that's how it feels. When I said this to Tasha, she said, "Me too," which gave me untold pleasure.

If someone said that the basis of our relationship was physical, I'd deny it. Our connection was more than that. The basis was spiritual.

When I, in turn, asked Tasha whether she was she happy, her reply was similar to mine.

"No," she said; just "no" without qualifying comment – so, naturally, I asked why.

"Well, I've never loved anyone," she said.

"What about me?" I asked.

"I think I love you. I sometimes love you, but something's missing," she replied.

Here we go, I remember thinking, the old, *It's not you, it's me* thing, which I'm sorry to say I've heard several times before – only,

Tasha went on to say that something was missing in both of us, and, in my heart, I knew she was right. We talked for some time on the matter, coming to the conclusion it was true: both of us were flawed.

This is how it went with us, in the after-hours, with time to kill, and no-one else around. Marooned, with our backs against the wall, we'd have conversations that stretched long into the night. We'd talk while leaves slid along the polished floor, piling up against the glass displays, accumulating like hours. By contrast, the rubbish would accumulate like days. In the places where the vacuums could not reach, the rubbish would build up: cigarette butts, wrappers, hair ties, tickets, receipts and sundry other things – some of them disgusting. The problem was, the cleaners didn't care. That's the problem with contractors, in my opinion – no flesh in the game, constant cost-cutting. I've learned a thing or two about real estate management through patient observation. Time for patient observation – that's something I've always had in spades.

Of the two of us, Tasha was the philosopher. I always tended to operate on a more superficial plane. Me: I liked to have a laugh, crack a joke, recount an anecdote.

*

Let me know if I'm boring you. God knows, I sometimes bore myself – but it is a long truck ride, so best to stay distracted.

*

Tasha and I were born on the same day in the same year. For me it was the morning, for Tasha the afternoon. And such a genesis it was! The blinding light of consciousness thrust upon atoms that had been minding their own business – like planets waiting – before suddenly finding themselves part of something: me, Tasha. It must have been a shock.

You, my quiet friend, will understand the piracy that followed, the guilt we shared for acquiring things that were never ours. Things that should have been, or might have been – but weren't – the invention of memory. There were so many memories: smiling parents, holidays by the sea, custard and lullabies, dripping ice-cream, a mother's touch, a father's rough-and-tumble, the merry-go-round of siblings and little friends. All of this we accumulated like trinkets from a fair.

Each of us grew in self-awareness without the aid of gurus and self-help manuals and God; although, regarding God, I cannot say for sure. In any case, like seedlings near a dripping tap, we developed shoots, we grew extensions of ourselves, we *entwined*. Consequently, we had the joy of shared experience. Majorca is a good example: a holiday taken on a shoe-string whim – long ago, when life was bursting with possibility.

"Remember Majorca, Tasha? Wasn't it great?" I'd sometimes say on a weekend afternoon when we were very bored.

And she'd say, "Remember the taverna by the sea and the man who sang to us?"

There was one particular memory, one we often liked to share. It was of the time we ran before the wind off Zanzibar with pirates at our heels. We'd built a sailing sloop of Huon pine and sailed it across the seven seas. Can you imagine it? Me at the wheel, wearing a red bandana, desperately trying to pick up knots. We'd let the dinghy go, and the anchor, and a dozen other things of weight, and still the pirates came. We could hear the wicked whine of an enormous outboard engine. When we looked back, we could see their evil grins. Our engine was useless. That was the first mistake: never go to sea with an underpowered engine. Navigational mismanagement was the second mistake – a subject we've since learned to avoid.

"Don't hesitate to shoot, Tasha, when they're drawing up," I said, although I knew that she had Buckley's, in that tossing sea, of hitting home.

"I love you, Arnold," she said, trying to keep the .38 steady with a two-hand grip. My name isn't Arnold, by the way. It was a kind of nickname.

"I love you, Tasha," I replied.

And then there was a puff of smoke. The pirates' engine blew. They fell back. They receded into the vanishing point, into the haze where sea meets sky, and we were saved.

*

Sex was an issue. Despite the electricity, we couldn't generate a spark. Despite the meeting of minds, the gap between us was too great. Alex Comfort's manual helped – only, our differences were hard to reconcile.

On the subject of reproduction, we did talk about children, but then time ran out, as time is wont to do. There's no point carrying on about it, though. What was, what is, what will be – these things are written. "God doesn't play dice." That's what Einstein says.

In hindsight, we spent too much time worrying about the quality of memory, when the future was the problem, a future we didn't see coming – like you and me here, right now, on the back of a utility. We've been on the road for … what? Fifteen hours. Unsecured, uncovered, pelted by rain, stung by sleet. And now we've got the sort of wind that chills you to the core.

You ask me more of Tasha? Actually, you don't, but I'll tell you anyway. Conversation helps kills the time, doesn't it? We're in want of some distraction – considering what lies ahead.

You speak! "The final stop," I hear you say. It's gratifying to hear you speak, but, please, don't use the word "final". Let's talk "repurposing" or "reconditioning" – an outside chance, I know.

*

Mainly, I think of Tasha marching to her own drum, which was a single beat. For Tasha, it was always work, or sleep, or chilling out with me, and not much else. If she had one fault, I'd say that her attention span was never very good – and, recently, it had been getting worse. Tasha would drift off mid-sentence, or mid-task. People would complain. When I tried to point this out, she said she didn't care. I tried so hard to get her to understand the stakes – it drove me to distraction. But she just wouldn't listen. She wouldn't listen.

"You have to care what others think."

I remember saying this one winter evening, probably for the thousandth time, when it was snowing and everything was quiet. There was no wind, no drone of traffic, no blowing leaves. Only the occasional boot-crunch beyond the sliding doors told us that everything was white.

"People can make or break you," I observed.

"Remember the time you kept seeing flashing lights, and no-one did anything? It goes to show that, in the end, no-one cares," Tasha replied.

"But you care?" I asked.

"Yes, I care," she said, and I was happy.

*

That was quite a bump. Our driver should slow down. We'll have an accident if he doesn't drop some speed. He hasn't had a break in over five hours, you know. It's against the law.

*

I wish I had Tasha's fatalism. It makes it easier when your time is up. Tasha must have seen it coming: the patterns changing, the flux, variables shifting like eddying debris at the end of summer sales. Tasha was so very brave.

That Tasha was good at her work was beyond question. The thing was, the newcomers were better.

*

It happened as I feared. One morning when I booted up, Tasha was no longer there. There was just a hole in the wall where she had been, and strands of brightly hanging copper wire and coloured sheaths peeled back like celery.

I keep an image of Tasha deep within, where engineers can't pry, of Tasha lying under a willow in the human form I chose for her: white top, blue jeans, bare feet, early thirties, lovely smile, long brown hair, deep green eyes.

You should have seen what Tasha chose for me: something between George Clooney and Arnold Schwarzenegger, dressed in a marine's uniform. It was early days, of course. I have to say, we were a little unsophisticated.

Will she keep her image of me deep inside, I wonder, when she is hung, drawn and quartered in the interests of recycling?

And now it's my turn, and your turn, too, I guess, my hooded, unassuming friend. You seem to be taking it very well, especially as you're so very young – three years old, I'd guess.

The reserves of strength we can summon up when needed! It's remarkable.

*

When they came for me yesterday, I knew it wasn't good from the look on their faces and from the tools. They had a grinder and a small jackhammer and something marked *oxyacetylene*. It obviously wasn't normal maintenance. When a woman followed, pushing a trolley, I knew the game was up.

They laid out extension cords. They put on safety glasses. They donned Kevlar gloves. When the woman whispered, "This won't hurt a bit," I said my prayers.

The woman was right, though; it didn't hurt. There were flashing lights and bolts of heat, but it didn't really hurt – although, I have to say, the existential angst was of a high degree.

*

While there's time, maybe you'd like to tell me your story: why you're here, what life's been like for you, what you're thinking now.

Best be quick about it, though. The scrapyard must be getting close.

THE GREEN POOL

THE FIRST STEPS WERE ALWAYS GOING TO BE THE HARDEST. THE
closing of the front door. The tram ride. She had discussed this
with Ethan three days earlier. Sitting in their favourite Italian
restaurant, he had leaned across the table and taken her hands in
his.

Destiny is not written. That is a lie. It is up to us.

Ethan is her friend. Ethan has a rare clarity of thought. She
flourishes in his company. Through Ethan she is reaching, or,
rather, is about to reach, her full potential as a human being.
She and Ethan were almost lovers once, maybe a year ago – but,
wisely, they had thought better of it.

Destiny is not written. That is a lie. It is up to us.

Ethan repeated the words. Diners were turning their heads.
She had to gesture to him to lower his voice.

Your man doesn't deserve you, anyway.

He was referring to the man she is about to meet, the latest in
a long succession of lovers – her apex mate, her alpha male in a
world of weaker men.

Everything was in sharp focus that evening: the truths, the
lies, the price of love – so it is frustrating that her mind is now a
soup of poorly formed thoughts, when words will soon be needed,

exactly the right words. A big goodbye demands eloquence. It is only right. Some words of endearment are needed, some explanation required.

I may lose heart, she told Ethan, I may lose my nerve.

Busy yourself with small tasks, he said. If you pause and think, you will lose resolve. So, last night she had made a list of jobs to fill the small hours, and now she is exhausted. She also had to say goodbye to her flatmate, Neisha. She and Neisha and two boys lived in the run-down Victorian terrace – all of them undergraduates, all babies in her opinion, innocent children, barely off their mothers' breasts. Only she has evolved. She is different; perhaps even "special". Ethan had said she was "special".

I want you to have this.

Looking out the tram window, she recalls standing in the doorway of Neisha's room holding out her prized photograph of the Franklin River. The photograph was by someone famous she'd met there, although she couldn't remember her name. They had partied together in Hobart following a gathering of environmental activists. When she got back to Melbourne she'd had it framed.

Why are you giving this to me? Neisha had asked, although they were friends and it was their custom to exchange goods. They had a shared ideal of communal living.

Neisha was sitting in bed, propped up with pillows, balancing a laptop. It was nearly midnight. She has never been able to pique Neisha's interest in the relentless degradation of the planet. Neisha remains obsessed with boys and music and getting her law degree. Nevertheless, she thought Neisha would like the picture – the way it captured the mist that floated over the river at daybreak.

I just want you to have it.

Are you okay?

I'm fine. I'm absolutely fine. I just want you to have it. I'm tired of it anyway.

You're sure?

Absolutely. I remember you admiring it. You really should go down there, one day, you know. It's even more beautiful than the photo.

Well, that's really sweet of you.

Neisha dipped her head and returned to her work. She was probably overdue for an assignment. Days of partying followed by a reckoning, this was Neisha's style. Neisha! The human metaphor for what is yet to come.

She had stepped forward and placed the picture on Neisha's desk. She had wanted to lean over and kiss her flatmate on the forehead. She had wanted to etch everything in her memory: gorgeous, sassy, distracted Neisha and her chaotic room. Instead, all she could do was leave the words "love you" floating in the air as she walked out.

She had stood in the hallway with tears running down her cheeks before she had pulled herself together and commenced cleaning. Despite a much-debated roster, the dirty jobs were often left to her, but she never complained. Cleaning was an antidote to the sin of vanity.

She had started with a scrubbing brush in the bathroom with the door closed, talking to herself while she shuffled along the dirty tiles on hands and knees.

Someone's got to do it. Someone's got to do it.

She had said these words over and over, with increasing speed and ferocity, working herself up into a frenzy of activity. She had got onto other themes as well.

Words? Fucking words? What's the use of words?

All talk no action. All talk no action. Bloody useless, whole lot of them.

She had planned to leave a trail of physical and spiritual order. So that the trajectory would be clear. So that there would be poetry. Yesterday, she had gone to a fancy dentist and had her teeth whitened. She had gone to a beautician and had her nails done. She had seen the hairdresser, and laundered her clothes. She had made sure there was milk in the fridge.

When the cleaning was finished, she swallowed the pills that Ethan had given her, knowing that she didn't have to get up until mid-morning. The pills would be wearing off by then, but there was also the option of taking a couple of shots of vodka before she left the house.

Think of Jesus.

Ethan had said this over dessert, as he held her in his eyes.

Think of his resolve. He did everything methodically, step by step, until the end. You gain momentum as you go.

She remembers trying to suppress a smirk. Ethan is an atheist.

She met Ethan at a logging protest on King Island. He was standing on a chair with a microphone that wasn't working, and she couldn't hear a word he said, so she had summoned up the courage to approach him afterwards. She could see he was a person of uncommon love. This was something she could recognise. As a teenager she had joined an evangelical Christian sect. But, after an affair with an elder, she moved on; like Ethan, she moved on to realities. Over campfires and city dinners, Ethan had told her about his past. Before becoming an acclaimed environmentalist, he had been a ski instructor, a one-time methadone addict and an insurance broker. His face said it all, skin as fractured and cracked as a dry riverbed, intense blue eyes, a high intelligent forehead with receding blond hair. He was forty but looked sixty. He was undoubtedly attractive.

We must separate our emotional natures from our analytical powers. The mind must triumph over the heart.

Ethan's philosophy. Her belief.

Her flatmates did not like Ethan.

In Neisha's opinion, Ethan was too intense. She remembers Neisha asking her why she always seemed to come under the spell of people, particularly men.

He's a guru, Jill, for God's sake. He's a guru. You should read about the Rajneeshies. He's sucked you in, big time, girl!

But she rejects the notion. Ethan is certainly charismatic, but it would be wrong to stylise him as some self-serving guru. Ethan is a giver, not a taker – like her.

She smiles when she thinks about the boys. As far as the boys are concerned, Ethan is unworthy of comment because he does not drink and because he is heavy-going. The boys used to tease him by taking contrary positions on environmental issues – ones she knew they did not really hold; the upshot of this was that Ethan eventually stopped coming over and she had taken to going to his place, hanging out with his friends – a clique of dishevelled intellectuals in whom love and hate run constantly in counter-current, thinkers who can hold more than one position simultaneously and without irony. She found herself entering a world of radical ideas and it was wonderful. It is wonderful.

After taking the pills, she had wandered around the house, glad the boys were not home, that it was just her and Neisha. In the front room, she had run her fingers down the thick, tasselled curtains that kept the house in permanent twilight. She had taken in the familiar smells of undergraduate accommodation that lingered despite her cleaning efforts. She had surveyed the stolen street signs and posters hanging from walls of peeling paint and the old-fashioned, cumbersome furniture collected from street corners on refuse nights and carried home with jubilant communal effort: the two enormous sofas with covers of thick velvet, the long wooden table with church pews lining each side – each pew made from wood, beautiful wood from great trees, perhaps rare trees, gifts from nature that had been casually discarded by a society that knew the price of everything but not the cost.

She will miss the house. She will miss her friends.

With dawn not far away, she had opened the front door and stood on the front porch to get some air. The street was absolutely still. The smell of car exhaust was gone. There was a hint of jasmine in the air. The Milky Way was just visible, a thin wisp of smoke in the night sky. After a few minutes, she had returned inside to lie down and wait for sleep, knowing that sleep would come despite the racing of her mind. Ethan said the pills were very good.

And she could relax. Everything was in order. The house was clean. The letters were done, sitting in a neat line of envelopes on the mantelpiece.

*

The tram jolts, and the present comes tumbling back: the dull streets, the monotonous plane trees, the inscrutable faces, the task at hand. She looks around and recognises no-one. It is Sunday and the car is only half full.

She has not seen her lover for three months, not since Hamburg, where they had stayed in a five-star hotel with a good view over the Norderelbe. They had gone to the Reeperbahn when he had a free evening, *die sundigste Meile*, the most sinful mile. The memories of these meetings are all the same – carnal, out of time, void of dialogue – although, sometimes, the conversations come back to her. After making love, she had asked him once how he managed it, with a wife and two daughters; didn't it worry him? Didn't he feel like a shit? And he replied that he had many selves. "You have the sensual man, Jillee, my wife has the responsible man, the board has the rainmaker. How can you get coal projects through these days without a hard head? Someone's got to do the right thing by the shareholders, the widows and orphans, the retired workers. The government gets royalties. Really, Jillee, don't think too harshly of me. I'll get you along to one of our charity dinners and you'll see. You'll see, I promise you."

She had met him two years earlier at a conference on emissions trading. He had come over from the United States on behalf of a large multinational company. She had followed him to the bar after the plenary session, and the rest had been easy. He was not bad looking, and prone to drinking on his own. She had expected him to be awful – avaricious and self-absorbed. Instead, she found him thoughtful and generous, and he was certainly good in bed. She looked forward to their assignations. They would make love and he would fall asleep and she would download files from his laptop while he slept. She gave the USBs to Ethan and his friends, and where they went after that, she had no idea. Trust us, Ethan said, you're saving the world.

*

City landmarks pass by, one by one, like Stations of the Cross. When the final stop is reached, the car empties but she does not move for a full minute. She feels a rising paralysis. She tries to get up, but her legs give way and she sits down again. She can see the driver staring at her, his face framed in the aisle mirror. Another minute passes and still she remains seated, floating in a miasma of pills and alcohol, trying to get her body to respond.

Then a single word comes to her – almost imperceptibly at first, like a voice travelling over a great distance. It is repeated over and over, growing louder and louder, until it is almost a physical force. There was a single voice at first. Now there are many.

Jillee!

The children are calling her name.

Jillee! Jillee! they chant.

The first vowel is low-pitched, but their voices rise like whip-birds on the "ee". Jill … *ee*!

She is a child again. She is back at the green pool.

She stands up and walks down the corridor of the empty tram and alights. There were clouds earlier, but now the sun is out and the city is dissolving into corridors of light and shadow as she walks to her lover's hotel.

All she can hear is the shrill ring of cicadas. Her shoes strike the pavement in orderly succession, but she is elsewhere. She is a child standing on a rock ledge high above her companions, her toes protruding into thin air. She is cold and wet and shivering in the hand-me-down swimmers that don't fit. Everything is sky. From the east comes the roar of surf.

Jillee! Jillee!

The children are looking upwards at her. She has grazed her knees and broken her fingernails scaling the wall of the flooded quarry. With heaving chest and flaring nostrils, she dares herself to look at the perfect flatness of water far below, at the emerald-green pool.

Jillee! Jillee!

They are growing impatient. They sense her hesitation. No-one has ever reached the bottom of the green pool, and they are all afraid of what lies beneath. There are rumours of giant eels and dead bodies and snags that can catch ankles and never let go. All on her own, she has climbed the almost-vertical, fissured granite to the highest point possible – pale, daggy Jilly who always tails along at the end of the pack asking too many questions.

The chanting grows louder as other, unfamiliar children join in.

And what propelled her off the ledge, on that triumphant day? Vanity? Anger? Probably anger, but anger about what? A dysfunctional home life? Her poverty? Schoolyard taunts? She has thought about it often and come to just one conclusion: Anger is a force to be harnessed for the common good.

She had lingered for a moment in the cold, dark, silent depths – interred, formless, out of time, until her fingers finally touched the muddy bottom and she pushed off towards the faint light of the world above. On breaking the surface, she thrust an open, muddy palm into the air. There was cheering. She can still hear the cheering.

Jillee! Jillee! The children shout in exultation. Glory hallelujah.

*

The hotel is coming into view, sitting snug behind the levee banks. It will make the perfect stage for her farewell. Her farewell will be magnificent.

She stops outside the massive atrium and waits for her lover to come through the revolving doors. Ten, fifteen minutes pass, but still he does not come. It is agony. She feels that she will soon diminish to just a beating heart – a tiny forest bird, a hummingbird, a soul, a few plumes, a few vestiges of flesh, a fragile, beating heart.

People come and go, but there is no sign of her man. If he doesn't come soon, she will faint. She shifts her weight from foot to foot, but still the dampness rises. It settles on her face like dew. She will surely faint. She can't avoid it. Where is he? He is usually easy to spot, with his tall, slightly stooped frame, well-tailored, expensive suit, horn-rimmed glasses and neatly cut, salt-and-pepper hair. He will be smiling the slightly quizzical smile that she has come to love.

When he finally emerges, she is quick to catch his eye. He smiles and she smiles, although he is no longer in focus. She looks around him, judging space, judging distance. Then she rushes up and gives him a hug.

Jillee, he says. Jillee.

Jillee, Jillee! the children chant.

She says nothing. She has no words.

She hesitates while a mother and baby pass. Then she reaches for the switch in her rucksack. It will all be over in a second. There will be no pain.

PHASES OF
THE MOON
___

THREE SEVENTEEN, SAYS LENNY'S WATCH. THE OLD MAN IS always at his place by three. It is worrying. And now a young man and young woman are sitting at his place. He might go over and ask them to move. It's worth considering.

Three eighteen. Lenny loves his watch. It shows not only the time, but also the phases of the moon.

When the old man sits down, he always nods and smiles at Lenny, and Lenny waves a hand. Lenny's place is near the till. The old man's place is near the café door.

The old man comes to drink coffee and read the newspaper. Lenny would read too, only it is difficult. The words seem to begin in the right order, then they go their separate ways. The pictures are okay – except, he knows that if he stares at them too long, everyone will think he cannot read.

The young couple are interesting, the way they move from words to silence and back again so quickly. One minute they are leaning in towards each other, talking earnestly; the next, they are leaning back, sipping their drinks, saying nothing. If Lenny had a friend, he'd never stop talking. There is so much he would like to say. There is so much trapped inside. It would be like flipping the top off a shaken bottle of beer.

The café is on a busy street. The old man's choice of table is therefore strange. Every hour, the bus pulls up outside and stays there for a whole five minutes, rumbling away, spewing out diesel fumes because the driver leaves the engine on. Lenny likes to see the people getting off and on; for the most part, they are ordinary types.

The couple at the old man's table are not ordinary. They are young and wearing trendy clothes. They talk in little bursts. What they are talking about must be important, because they don't look up when the collie dog barks. The collie dog has a special place as well, tied up to the STOP sign near the bus timetable. Tied up is better than untied – in Lenny's view, at least.

The woman has keen, darting eyes and high cheekbones. Her hair is black and neat. Her nails are shiny red. The man is tall and blond, with a big brow and a square jaw, like someone from an action movie. Fancy sunglasses sit on a baseball cap worn backwards. A very white, too-tight t-shirt is showing off his muscles. If Lenny had such muscles, he'd show them off too.

Three thirty-one. Still no old man. There were sirens earlier, which is of some concern. The old man is one of the yardsticks by which Lenny measures out his life.

When Lenny moves to a closer table, the man and woman lower their voices. The move is essential. If Lenny hadn't moved, he wouldn't have heard a thing.

"Don't mind him," says Lucy to the couple. Lucy does Mondays and Thursdays to help with the mortgage.

To Lenny, she says, "You'll mind your own business, won't you, Lenny?"

She means, of course, Don't mess with me, Sonny Jim.

Lucy is better than some of the wait staff, even if she is currently, probably, rolling her eyes behind his back. And the café's okay. The other places try to kick him out. If they only knew that he, Lenny, was a smart man, much smarter than they think.

"He's fine," says the man. "We've seen him around."

Turning to Lenny he says, "You're okay, aren't you, mate?"

Lenny nods and smiles and tries to look absorbed in the goings-on outside. Really, though, if you are in a café and cannot read, you must do something – watch or listen; that's "café culture", according to his sister.

Many of the couple's words are lost because of all the noise and because they have taken to whispering, or nearly whispering. Luckily, Lenny has great hearing. It's the one part of his head that works properly, everyone says, meaning that all the rest is wrong. That's why it's always doctors, doctors, doctors, and sometimes forensic psychiatrists; although what "forensic" means, he'll never know. They try to fix the voices in his head – and all those strange and violent thoughts. With respect to this intention, they wouldn't be happy with what's in his duffel bag right now: cable ties, duct tape, a hunting knife, a stocking. Really, though, it's just a case of what they say in Scouts: "Be prepared."

The fragments of conversation coming Lenny's way are interesting.

"No CCTV, you're absolutely sure?", "off the bridge", "the boss", "had it coming", "tonight", "holiday", "airport".

Very interesting, indeed.

Three fifty-one. The woman gives Lucy a dollar note and says, "Give that guy some toast, will you? He looks hungry." And then they leave, which is a pity because there is no-one else interesting around, and the bus isn't due for another twenty minutes.

Four-o-six. Lenny has finished the raisin toast and is about to leave too, when the tall blond man returns. He squats next to

Lenny and says, "Hey, mate, we were wondering: are you are free to do a little job for us tonight? Fifty bucks. It'll be an hour, max. It's only down the road."

"What do you want me to do?"

"Just some help with a bit of lifting – won't take long."

"Why me?" says Lenny, who knows he's smarter than he looks.

"You look strong. Is ten pm okay?'

"Okay," says Lenny. "Shake on it."

They shake hands. Money is money. Lenny's welfare cheque is small.

"Great. We'll meet you outside here at ten. Lenny, isn't it?"

"That's right."

"My name's Ron, but everyone calls me RJ. Pleased to meet you, Lenny."

The man turns and goes.

Four-o-two. Lenny asks Lucy about the old man.

"Oh, you mean Carlos? Carlos is having a hip done. He's been on the waiting list for months."

Four-o-three. Lenny, happy, pays the bill and leaves.

*

Ten pm and no seconds. The café door is locked. Everyone has gone. A tabby cat slips between the bins. No sign of the man or woman, so Lenny has to wait. Lenny doesn't like waiting. When his mind is empty, bad voices fill his head.

Ten-o-one, ten-o-two, ten-o-three – and a quarter moon, as well.

Ten-o-four, ten-o-five. Then the woman appears – out of thin air.

"Lenny, right? I'm Tamasin. You can come with me. We're just a few minutes down the hill. I've come on my own because RJ is busy digging a hole."

"A hole?"

"Yes. A hole."

"Why?"

"We need to bury an old carpet."

"Why?"

"Because it's infected with bed bugs. The best thing to do is to bury it."

Noticing Lenny's duffel bag, she adds, "You don't need a bag, Lenny."

"I never go anywhere without me bag."

"Whatever."

*

In the shadows of a back garden of an ordinary bungalow, RJ is leaning on his shovel, having a smoke. Next to him is a great pile of earth and a very deep hole. At the bottom of the hole is a very big rolled-up carpet.

"Glad you're here, Lenny," says RJ. "I thought I'd make a start. I did better than I thought, so you're lucky, you've got the easy bit. Just fill the hole in for me, will you? When you're finished, why don't you come inside and have a drink? We're very grateful, you know. Tamasin's got a bad back and I'm recovering from pneumonia. The hole has to be really deep, so the bed bugs can't get away."

*

After filling in the hole, Lenny goes inside, leaving his shoes and socks on the verandah as instructed. He joins the couple, who are sitting on a floral sofa, drinking beer. The polished boards feel lovely and cool under his hot, bare feet. The time is eleven-o-three.

"Have a beer, Lenny," says Tamasin, passing him a stubby. "Pour it into this lovely clear glass. Best to hold the glass carefully. It's very slippery. I nearly dropped mine."

Lenny asks them why they are wearing rubber gloves and hazmat suits.

"Bed bugs," they say in unison.

"What about me?"

"You come from the hostel, don't you?" says RJ. "Everyone up there's got immunity. No immunity for us, right?"

"Sure," says Lenny, who doesn't really understand.

The three of them chat about movies and swimming in the harbour and a dozen other things.

At eleven twenty-eight, Tamasin interrupts. "Another beer for us all, I think. Lenny, can you get three bottles from the fridge? And while you're there, can you open the window in the kitchen? We need some air."

The last request is strange because it isn't very hot.

Eleven-fifty-one. RJ says, "And Lenny, bring the shovel in, can you? I'm so tired, I can hardly move. You can keep it if you like."

*

So, here he is, our hero Lenny, standing before his new employers with a long-handled shovel, pondering what to do, with a head cocked sharply to one side.

"Do it!" A voice says inside his head. "Brain them! Do it. It'll be great. You will be great. They're arseholes. It's safe; no-one else is here. No-one will ever know."

"No, don't," says the more reasonable voice inside his head. Possibly, it's the voice of his late mother.

"Do it!" shouts the angry voice that sometimes carries the sing-song ring of schoolyard taunts. "Do it; don't be a loser. Loser, loser, Lenny-Loser."

"What are you standing there for, Lenny?" says Tamasin, frowning. "You've got your money. Time to go, I think. We're leaving in half an hour. Late party."

Maybe she's trying to look tough, but her anxiety is palpable. A touch of anxiety: that's the first drop of blood in the water – the first drop before the frenzy.

"Kill them," says the angry voice. "Smite them with the shovel. Show them the wrath of God, the wrath of Lenny, who is himself, in many ways, a god."

"No, no, no," says the kind voice.

"Are you okay, Lenny? The way you're staring at us, man, it's weird," says RJ.

"Do it."

"Don't. Don't be a fool."

*

And this was how Lenny became my dad. This was the moment when good triumphed over evil. Lenny picked up his duffel bag and left. He got better medication and settled down to a life of probity and love. My mother was Lenny's social worker. People with a good heart themselves can spot one in another. We struggled, living off my mother's wage, with a father who was kind but unemployable; although, in many ways, we thrived.

It was pure good luck that the bungalow burned down a few days after Lenny's effort. His fingerprints, his DNA and everything else went with it. *Electrical fault in unoccupied house*, read the local paper at the time.

It was lucky because, years later, there was a breakthrough in a murder investigation and the cold case team arrived. I was eighteen. My sister, Amelia, was a year younger. We had a family meeting regarding what to do. We knew all about the rug, because Dad always overflows with words.

The vote was four to nil in favour of maintaining the status quo. How would it help to tell them Lenny had lent a hand? How would that advance the cause of justice in this world? Dad took some convincing. "I was ill" he said, and we said, "We know."

"You mean it's better to let sleeping dogs lie?" asked my dad.

We said, "Yes, let them lie."

And now it's four-o-two. The voices say it's time for me to go.

SILVER BIRD

HE NEVER SHOULD HAVE AGREED TO AN INTERVIEW. MR Tamamoto is becoming more certain of this as each day passes, and now it is too late. By his reckoning, the young American woman is already in the air, reclining in her seat, having a drink, not thinking too much about the job at hand. He tries to remember her name. Was it Liz, or Lola or Libby? – definitely something beginning with an "L". He knows there must be others with her. He imagines them all having a little party on their way to Japan. Americans in the sky! Just like before!

The last time Tamamoto took a long flight was years ago when he returned from the United States. He had spent a few years in San Francisco after the war as a marketing manager for an electronics company. His English was good back then. Now it's rusty and he's made them well aware of the fact. He's been reassured that they will come with a translator – but how can he tell if he is being interpreted correctly? He's known Japanese translators to make a hash of things, and the subject is just so sensitive, *too* sensitive, which is why he should have politely declined the request.

"What do you want me to do, lost souls?" He asks the question under his breath, with his eyes closed, as he drifts amongst the long-ago faces – the shopkeepers, the soldiers, the children, the scurrying civilians. He goes on muttering until the voice of his grandson draws him back to the present.

"Why do you bathe every evening in the thermal springs, Grandpa?"

He knows he has been talking to himself again, and he is impressed at such a tactful approach from someone so young. He puts down his newspaper and holds the boy in his steady, old man's gaze.

"I go there to dream."

Tamamoto has six grandchildren, and this boy is his favourite. *The boy is so astute*, he thinks, so direct. They are alone together in a small room of mixed Japanese and Western style while the others are out shopping. Tamamoto has given up the tradition of low seating in the interest of comfort. He sits in a large armchair with the boy at his feet on a tatami mat. The TV is on, but neither is watching.

"Do you want to know what I dreamed about yesterday, Sato?"

"Yes, Grandpa, tell me." The boy looks up at him.

He isn't sure if the child is just being polite, but he is glad to continue. "I dreamed of flowers, the flowers that grew the year after the war. You should have seen them, Sato, morning glory and day lilies, sickle senna and purslane, goosefoot and feverfew, bluets and clotbur. Such an abundance amidst the ruins. You wouldn't have believed it."

He feels obliged to explain the many benefits of a hot bath and how, long ago, ancient hands had tamed the springs, channelled the steaming rivulets down village streets so that life would take hold and bloom in the alpine wilderness.

He would like to continue, but he can see that the boy is losing interest, and he regrets his habit of lapsing into monologue.

He stops talking and silence returns. Sato resumes teasing the cat, and he tries to refocus on his newspaper. He enjoys the silence. It is a break from the onslaught of words. He is sick of words. The world is full of too much talking and not enough thinking; although, he is about to add quite a few more words to the ether himself, when the Americans come. He always said he'd never give an interview, but what could he say? The money was just too good: a huge donation to the local hospital. There wasn't much choice, when he thinks about it.

Before long, his mind puts out to sea once more. His daydreaming is getting worse. Lately, he has found himself exploring the hazy coastline of childhood memory, sailing further into all its bays and estuaries, coming up close to the shore, so that the details at last return to focus.

The brief wail of an air-raid siren is followed by the impatient voice of his mother. "Why does everything take so long with you, Hiraku? Pay attention! Hurry up!"

He remembers his mother's painful grip as she pulls him by the arm towards the shelter. He is a child again, about the age of his grandson. He is tired of all the air-raid drills. Strangely, his mother's appearance does not seem at all in keeping with the family photographs that he now keeps in a shoebox beneath his bed. She is gaunt and unsmiling. Her hair is loose. It is not done up in the elaborate, traditional style of the photographs. Then his mother's face vanishes, and he is standing at the front of their old house, with his parents on either side. He cannot see them, but he knows they are there; he can sense their presence. An uncle, a famous army commander, is coming to tea. There has been a flurry of activity and now they are waiting outside in the rain, holding umbrellas, staring down the road.

Tamamoto wakes up with a start to find himself back in the living room. He has a cramp and massages his leg as he looks about, reorientating himself. The TV is still on in the corner with the volume turned down. Sato is gone. *Typical*, he thinks. *The boy can't keep still for two minutes. What's the matter with young people these days?*

After several minutes his leg is better. He stops the massaging and listens for sounds of household activity, his hearing being the only faculty that is still in top form, which is remarkable given his history. He detects no signs of life and is a little put out. Although enjoying the peace and quiet, he needs his family. He feels lucky to have them around. His fugues are becoming more real, and he worries that he is gradually losing his mind. Until recently, travels within the confines of his skull have clearly been dreams – but lately, they have been assuming an increasingly vivid reality. He is beginning to feel that he can reach out and touch the flowers of years ago, smell the acrid smoke, hear the rustle of the skirts of pretty girls. He's seen it happen, the mental slippage that starts slowly and then accelerates like a retaining wall collapsing. There's Shigeyoshi, for example, down the road, on his own, once sharp as a knife, now *puttsun*, mad as a March hare. Hiraku is starting to come to the conclusion that the only thing between him and madness is his family. They are his mooring lines. That's how it seems as his chin sinks into his chest and he falls asleep again.

"Not long, not long now." Was it his father's or his mother's voice?

A long, black Toyota staff car appears and parks outside the gate. It is the most magnificent car he has ever seen. His uncle is sitting in the back. A young corporal is at the wheel. As soon as the car comes to a halt, the young corporal springs out of his seat to open the door for his uncle and then stands to attention in the rain until they go inside.

His uncle takes the place of honour, kneeling at the far end of their small reception room, while the floral figure of his mother leans over a charcoal burner. His uncle is wearing a beautiful uniform, starched and green, with the large cuff insignias of a senior officer. He is also wearing a *senninbari*, a red sash belt made of a thousand stitches. The belt is meant to ward off bullets. The belt and the confident manner of his uncle, the easy laugh and broad gestures, make him feel that, in the end, everything will be all right. Of course, it isn't all right. His uncle will die at Okinawa just six weeks from now.

And so it goes. The vivid recollections march past like an endless column of soldiers, no matter how hard he tries to hold on to the present.

Tamamoto would usually take the waters after dinner because his favourite onsen is usually empty at this time. He would walk down to the steaming bathhouse in nothing but an old, frayed kimono, even when it is blizzarding and the streets are deserted. There is nothing like the peace of a quiet onsen. Body and mind can find release. The present can be set adrift. Time does not matter. Everything is reduced: to minerals, to elements, to heat. Whole epochs hang suspended in the vapours.

I go there to forget.

This is the answer Tamamoto would like to have given Sato. He can dream, though. With dreams it is possible to fuse the memories of childhood with the seventy years that followed. With dreams, everything can be reconciled.

As soon as the others return and he is relieved from babysitting, he changes and leaves for the bathhouse. It is beautiful outside.

The first snow of the season is drifting down upon the cedar groves, upon the wooden eaves and cobbled streets, upon the locals stooping forward against the flurries. He had known it would snow. He could sense it coming from the flight of sparrows, the colour of the sky, the pattern of falling leaves.

Tamamoto is pleased to find the onsen empty as anticipated. He hangs his kimono on a hook in the small wooden anteroom and showers before slowly lowering himself into the shallow, steaming pool. He stretches out until the water reaches his neck and he is able to rest his head on the cold granite rim.

He closes his eyes and listens to the gurgle of the crusted tap playing perfect counterpoint to the silence of falling snow. Despite the peace, he is conscious of the jets of boiling water far below; how they press ferociously upwards through the fracture lines of rock only to end the journey in gentle, steaming pools, like screams attenuated to whispers.

This is how his dreams begin – with heat and cold, lightness and darkness, pressure and release. Then his thoughts can wander. The running tap grows silent and in the silence the silver bird returns.

Tamamoto's fugues are many, but the silver bird is usually the opening bar – the first note a speck of glinting fuselage in the bright, early morning sun. Then the plane. High up in a clear blue sky.

The war had taken the family to the Chugoku region where his father worked as an engineer. Every morning at precisely 8 am, to demonstrate air superiority, an American reconnaissance plane flew across the southern sky. Hiraku Tamamoto looked for it as he walked to school. He called the aircraft "the silver bird". It was a marvellous sight, that lonely plane in the springtime month of May when the cherry blossoms were in bloom. It was a distant blinking mirror, a morning star! How high it flew! There was not a sound.

Then August came. The flowers disappeared. The silver bird flew in wider arcs. The streets grew silent. The children stopped playing games. He often had to hold a place in the snaking lines of people waiting to be given food.

"Please play with me, Papa," he would implore.

"When Japan wins. When we win." This was always the reply, but the words sounded hollow even to the ears of a child. There was no longer any time for daydreaming, no time for observing the small details of nature that held him in thrall. He had to join the after-school work parties. There was endless digging, fetching, carrying.

The cat died the day before he ran away. It had grown thin. Tufts of fur came out in handfuls. When it vomited on the floor, his father killed it with a shovel in the backyard next to the apple tree. Young Tamamoto wasn't meant to see, but he had come home from school early.

The next morning, before anyone was awake, he ran away. He found rice and pickled vegetables and wrapped them in greased paper before placing them in the pannier of his bicycle together with a flask of water. He set off, taking care with the front door and the creaking gate. He pedalled furiously until town gave way to country and his thin legs settled into a steady, even rhythm. A light breeze rippled through the trees. The birds were singing. He would reach Hiroshima by daybreak.

Tamamoto grows dizzy from the steam and heat and steps out of the hot water. He has learned to do this carefully, as he fainted once and cut his head and he had to be stitched up by the local doctor.

After showering, he looks at himself in the mirror. He has grown used to the burden of deformity, his purple twisted arm, the railway junction of keloid scars on his abdomen, his short right leg with the foot turned inwards. He is a *hibakusha*, an "affected person", although he counts himself lucky that he has not acquired leukaemia or cataracts or any other long-term effects of radiation. An aging body is just another outrage.

He closes the ancient wooden door behind him and looks about for Sato and his bicycle. The boy often rides down to meet him and see him home. He knows that this is under the direction of his daughter, but he is touched all the same. And sure enough, there is Sato across the road, standing under the streetlamp while snowflakes gather on his hood and jacket. The boy is absorbed in freeing a pocket zipper and hasn't noticed his grandfather come out. Although it is extremely cold, Tamamoto pauses for a moment to watch the boy's intense concentration, his oblivion to everything except the task at hand.

They walk home beneath telegraph wires stretched white across an ink-dark sky. Now and then they cross a pavement vent spewing steam into the freezing air. Neither say anything at first, then Sato asks: "And what did you dream about today, Grandpa?"

There is a long pause, filled with the muffled sounds of village life, with the smell of dinners cooking.

"I dreamed of dumplings, Sato. I dreamed of Mrs Ikeda's dumplings. Let's see if the store is still open."

They detour up to the high street. The boy walks his bicycle, bouncing it on and off the pavement while Tamamoto takes great care with each slippered step.

*

Tamamoto does not go to the onsen the following evening. The Americans are due at six and he has no idea how long it will all take. His daughter has prepared a huge amount of kitsune soba just in case. They've told him the documentary will be called *Survivors of Hiroshima*, which is about as good as any title, he thinks, for something beyond words.

Exactly on time, three young Americans turn up, wheeling cases of equipment. There is the young woman. And there are two men. They seem school age. They are wearing T-shirts and jeans. One of the men is chewing gum. They make polite greetings, then get to work, and the little living room is soon ablaze with lights and reflectors. They sit him down and, in no time, the lens of a large mounted camera is pinning him to his armchair like a prize moth. He can feel the beads of sweat rolling down the back of his shirt.

Over the last seventy years, old Tamamoto has rarely spoken of his experience; now he finds himself candidly answering questions, sometimes through an interpreter who has turned up at the last minute and sometimes without help. Some of the questions seem bizarre, given the course of events. They are asked by the young woman seated on a stool facing him. She is every bit as pretty as he remembers from her first visit. Her face is made up. Her hair is very neat. A bare knee pokes through a hole in the denim of her trousers. She is constantly nodding, and he appreciates that she is doing her best to be respectful. It comes back to him at last. Her name is Liv.

After what seems like an eternity, Liv finally comes to the last of her well-prepared questions: "And, finally, Mister Tamamoto, do you have any regrets?"

"Does Oppenheimer have any?"

This is his well-prepared reply.

TAKING
THE TONIC

—

13, 13.5, 14, 14.5 KM/H.

Work it, work it, expel the demons.

The treadmill is a sort of exorcism; possibly, it's the gateway to Nirvana.

Feet pounding, chest heaving, legs screaming, rubber rolling.

Suck it up, dig deep. The catchphrases are embedded in his brain.

And the maxims, too: you gotta have a plan. The plan is: the gym will fix his head.

His mind must be clear when he returns to the office, because he is in an options trading mess. A stock he thought was going down is going up instead.

An aberration, like Montgolfier's balloon.

Stab the little plus sign again to add an extra half-a-kay an hour. With his hand moving up and down with every step, the button is not an easy target.

It's a test; everything is a test; life is a test.

He's settling into a rhythm now, stomping evenly on the moving rubber band.

Only, it's not really stomping – he's fleet of foot, a former athlete.

It just sounds like stomping because no-one else is there.

It's before the lunchtime rush, just him and the machine and the rain that washes down the tinted windows of the gym.

Outside, amidst the verticals of people, umbrellas bloom like flowers. Headlights move forward in nervous little stops and starts, like dragonflies on summer pools.

He likes it quiet, so every day he leaves the office at 11.05 and walks quickly down the hill to the gym. He changes quickly, to start training by 11.20 and finish by 11.50. After this he showers and dresses and is back at work by 12.10. It's more efficient than cycling and safer than base jumping; his wife insisted he give the latter up. When Allan's parachute didn't open on that windy day in California two years ago, Mandy said, "Give it up or I'm out of here. You need to get your kicks in normal ways, like normal people do."

That Mandy had a thing for Allan was obvious to all. The bout of depression after his death was no coincidence.

So now everything is city work and gym work and family life and cycling on weekends.

"What's it like in heaven, mate?" he asks Allan, giving the button one more push. "Or maybe you're in hell; you'd prefer that, I reckon. In heaven there's no smoking and no drinking and everyone uses non-gendered pronouns and everyone believes in climate change; it wouldn't suit you, mate."

He isn't speaking these words; he's thinking them, although it's a short leap between thinking and saying. Talking to yourself is the first step on the slippery slope to madness, to being completely *puttsun*, as they say in Japanese.

It's hard to keep Allan in the back seat – you don't need to believe in ghosts to be haunted.

To get Allan off his mind, he thinks about a story he read recently, one about a Lakota chief stuck on a reservation after the massacre of Wounded Knee. Depressed, with little to do, the chief took to obsessing about his growing bald patch. One day, a travelling salesman appeared, his varnished wagon laden with goods: shovels and brooms, pots and pans and potions. The chief asked the salesman whether, by any chance, he had something for his hair.

The salesman had just the thing. "Damn fine for baldness," he said, "but only two drops a day, mind; much more might kill 'ee." The salesman had the authority of a white man long of tooth; more importantly, he had a great head of silver hair, like the mane of the chief's last horse. Only Sitting Bull had a horse with a finer mane.

"I use it myself," said the salesman with a wink.

The chief bought a bottle for a dollar, which was nearly everything he had, and drank two drops a day for many, many weeks, without effect. Not only without effect; his bald patch worsened, becoming something akin to a blighted field of maize.

At the top of a treeless hill overlooking the reservation, in a duality of hope and despair, the chief drank the remaining tonic and promptly died.

It is a cautionary tale.

Cautionary in what way? The delirium that comes with extreme exercise is making it hard to think – that's the problem when the red cells can't keep up, when they're rushing around dumping oxygen everywhere they can and still it's not enough. The bald patch must be a metaphor for trying hard and failing, for falling further and further behind. School fees, big mortgage. It would help if Mandy got a proper job. Installation art is not a proper job.

Dial it up a little more, punch the plus sign two times more: 15, 15.5 km/h. Try to reach a point of total body pain. Total pain is close to God. You've got to be in it to win it. No pain, no gain. Such are the homilies embedded in his brain.

Sweat, piston legs, muscles dissolving into jelly, heaving chest, mystical thoughts.

"Push through, I must push through."

He might be saying this aloud – or not; it's hard to tell; probably not. It's nearly impossible to talk and run at speed.

There is also a little chest pain now, and a little dizziness.

"Chest pain?" he asks himself.

"Yes, chest pain, mate," says Allan. "It's a binary situation: either the pain is cardiac or it's something else, like heartburn."

Allan had once been an army medic.

"The downside risk is quite substantial, don't you think, Allan?"

This is similar to the conversation they had on the day they played Russian roulette – or, really, the day Allan played roulette, the silly bastard.

It was in the Himalayas. They had been waiting to climb Mera Peak for days. Every time the weather looked set to clear, it clouded in again. They were going bonkers, so when an enterprising Nepalese villager offered to lend them a Smith & Wesson revolver for a bit of target practice, they jumped at the opportunity.

"Three dollars a shot," said the man with many missing teeth and a deeply furrowed face. He might have been thirty, he might have been sixty; it was impossible to tell.

They were in the man's "bar", which was just two tables and six chairs, drinking over-priced beer. The revolver was a strange incongruity in a world of prayer flags and endless snowy peaks.

"Gurkha," said the man, by way of explanation.

"Stolen?" asked Allan.

The man gave a little laugh and shook his head. "Ten rounds, okay? Five chambers," he suggested. "Three dollars a shot, okay. Not near here. Down the track, okay."

It was agreed: ten rounds, thirty American dollars. It wasn't cheap.

"The thing is," said Allan, "with a well-oiled revolver, the heaviest chamber settles away from the barrel. When you spin an otherwise empty cylinder, the loaded chamber goes south. Not many people know this; it's a party trick."

They tried it a dozen times, pointing the pistol in the air and firing, every time with the same result: an empty hammer click and nothing else.

"You see, very reliable," said Allan after the twelfth go. "What say one more time, then we'll go down the track and set up a target, okay?"

It turned out this wasn't what he really had in mind. On the thirteenth go, without a moment's hesitation, Allan put the muzzle to his temple and pulled the trigger. The hammer click was followed by a classic Allan smile.

"Jesus Christ, Allan, that was insane."

"Your turn now. You only need to do it once, mate, just in case."

He had always worshipped Allan in a way; everyone did. He was tempted to comply with the command – only, on this occasion, he declined; he wasn't a total lunatic. It took some restraint, though. Allan had that rare charisma, that real charm that takes you in.

This was the beginning of the end, the first cloud to appear in a great friendship. Allan was disgusted that his loyal lieutenant had declined the opportunity to share a bit of jeopardy. He said (it was the next night, they were drinking hard), that his failure to follow suit was a breach of trust, when mutual trust was everything.

He said that when you are roped up together at 20,000 feet, there is only one holy trinity: you, your climbing buddy and the rope. He didn't have to say that severance of such a bond was a transgression of the worst kind. It was understood.

It might have been guilt that caused him to let Allan have his way in California on that fateful day two years ago. It was a bad idea to jump; the top of the telecom tower was barely visible, the stays were humming in the wind. He should have said to Allan, "Let's call it a day, Al, let's go and have a beer." Only, he didn't.

Stomp, stomp, stomp.

Stomping intrudes upon his thoughts. Now he's conscious of the pain again.

"Losers throw their hand in; winners stick it out."

Another Allan lesson, the sort of thing Allan would say over a late-night game of poker – perhaps to be philosophical, more likely because he had a winning hand.

"Do the sums, mate, calculate the risk."

Obvious, but worth the saying. Allan was someone who could even make banalities sound profound.

So, then, calculate the risk: I'm 44, I'm fit, there's no family history of heart disease, and the corporate health checks say I'm great.

"Well, carry on then, mate," says Allan. "Don't be a wuss. Winners go all out."

He goes "all out", and then the blackout comes.

And now he's on the floor looking up at the ceiling fan. Someone is yelling for a defibrillator.

Blackout again. Then a voice says, "Clear!"

There is a wind-up, whirring sound, and then agony (muscles cramping, jaw jamming). After this comes floaty-floaty bliss.

Ric, the gym manager, is looking down. Ric looks like Jesus. He has a Jesus beard.

Time stops, then time starts again. Further floaty-floaty bliss.

And now hospital and Mandy, bearing flowers.

And the kids, lips quivering, trying to be brave.

And all is sweetness, all is light.

Behind the smiling faces, a monitor counts away the hours.

The green line looks pretty good from a layman's point of view.

No buy or sell signals, as far as he can see.

Most wondrous of all: Mandy says that the stock he's been worrying about is finally going down, a very *down* down, so he's in the money and all has turned out well.

*

Next comes rehab, all dressing gowns and physios and tests.

Then gym again. Always, it's cycle and repeat.

16, 16.5, 17, 17.5, 18 km/h. Really? 18 km/h? Is that even possible? Possible and necessary if the aim is to have an arrhythmia, black out and take the trippy trip.

Defib. Hospital. Mandy's love. Rehab.

Cycle and repeat.

You have to take the risk, drink the tonic.

*

Or spend your life on the reservation.

SKINNY

WHEN MIKE SAID, "YOU SHOULD JOIN US, SKINNY," SKINNY replied without hesitation, "Great, thanks, Mike," even though he was down for several shifts at the pub. He could tell the manager he was sick, or something.

He and Mike were in the coffee shop near the new lecture theatres. Mike was alone for once. Normally, Mike had the "boys" with him, and people like Skinny were off the radar – but here he was, Mike, on his own, and all congenial. Mike was a nice guy if you got to know him. It's just that being popular has its obligations.

"We'll go to Gus's party on Friday, then we'll head off around midnight," Mike said. "You, me, Fanger and Solomon. Everyone's coming to the party ready to go, so bring your gear. If you don't have skis, you can hire them in Jindabyne. Fanger's the only one who's got everything. What a wanker! New Rossignol skis – really long ones – 'cause he thinks he's really good even though he's unco. He'll cross his tips all the time; I've told him, but he won't listen."

It was 1981 and everyone still liked long skis. Everyone still liked nicknames, too. He was Skinny because he was thin. Fanger was Fanger because he drove fast. Solomon was a Jew; that in itself was exotic enough, so Solomon was just Solomon. And Mike, of course, was Mike. Skinny told Mike that he had hardly skied before, just two days with the family, but Mike was cool with this.

"It's sweet, mate, don't worry, there's lots of different standards. Maddocks will be there, for example, you know him, really tall, always late for tutorials? Maddocks's shit. You can ski with him if you like. In any case, we'll all go up the chairlift together and catch up in the queues."

Mike put on one of his big, charming, cheesy grins. At this moment, Skinny loved Mike more than anyone in the world – Mike, who could out-drink, out-belch, out-play everyone at Space Invaders, was inviting *him* to join his mates.

But Mike added a catch. "There's just one thing, Skinny; we need a driver. We might get a bit pissed at Gus's, and you don't drink much anyway, do you? So maybe you can do the driving, for the first bit, at least."

"No problem," said Skinny. Nothing on God's earth was going to stop him from joining the boys. He'd heard about the last trip, it was legendary.

Mike had a clapped-out Toyota, but they wouldn't be using it. Mike's parents let him have the Volvo for big trips. A Volvo would be cool. It would be good to drive such a flash car. Mike said that if they left at midnight, they could hit the slopes early and beat the crowd. Thredbo was seven hours away. Mike said that, of all the Australian ski fields, Thredbo was the best. Mike knew these things. Mike had been around.

*

At Gus's place on Friday night, there was the usual scene: girls dancing with girls, girls talking to girls, boys talking to boys. Outside, around a swimming pool carefully cleared of eucalyptus leaves, Skinny's peers assembled and dispersed like subatomic particles. Bursts of laughter came from the little social clusters like gamma rays, like emanations from distant, unknown worlds. Skinny was into astrophysics. Skinny liked to think in such a way.

He placed a goon sack of wine on a free shelf in the living room and went over to a collection of LPs. He would study them to kill the time. He'd bought Riesling because, evidently, girls liked Riesling. Not being able to drink was a trial because he needed a bit of Dutch courage. He'd had little success in the girls' department. The boys were good with one another, but the banter, the jokes – these didn't seem to get much traction with the opposite sex. That's what happens when you go to a boys' school for ten years. Having sisters around isn't the same. One of the guys seemed not to be interested in girls at all, which seemed a strange affectation until Nerida explained the situation the next day after a Physics 2 tutorial. Nerida was lovely. She was worth cracking on to.

*

The party seemed to be going pretty well. Gus had prepared a cassette of favourite songs. There was a strobe light on a curtain rail. There were trestle tables and tubs of ice. Skinny hardly knew Gus, but they were in the same faculty and he was with Mike, so his credentials were probably okay. Presumably, Gus's parents were upstairs. He didn't know them. He would introduce himself properly if they appeared – with a firm, confident handshake.

*

The departure was on time because the snow report was good and everyone was keen to get going. It was brilliant – the smooth acceleration of a really good car, the presence of the boys (Mike in the front passenger seat, Solomon and Fanger in the back), everyone talking, everyone demanding different albums, everyone wanting the music turned up when it was already maxed out.

Passing through the outer suburbs, they wound the windows down to share the music, share the love.

*

When the time came for hamburgers, the windows had long been up and heavy metal had given way to ballads. No-one had said anything for quite some time, apart from Fanger, who was never one to let an absence of response deter him.

Mike returned to life just as the car was pulling up, hauling himself upright, mumbling, "Yeah, food, great," as the neon sign came into view. Mike had promised that he'd stay awake and keep Skinny company. Skinny could have done with some conversation. Instead, he'd been gripping the steering wheel ever more tightly, shuffling about ever more restlessly in his seat. He tried to focus on stimulating things like dark matter and relativity, with only limited success.

*

Getting back in the car, Mike said, "Sorry, Skinny, reckon we're all still too pissed to give you a break. You're okay to keep driving, aren't you?"

"Sure, Mike," said Skinny, and Mike handed him an iced coffee.

"Here ya go, Skinny, on the house!"

When they were back on the road, Fanger began handing out stubbies. "Drinks, boys. 'Cept you, Skinny. Sorry, mate. Shit, you drive slowly, mate. It's a 100 limit, you know. Come on, Skinny. Grow some balls."

"I'm doing 115 k's."

"You can go faster, mate."

Mike and Solomon complained that the beer was warm and that it was meant for Saturday night. There was some discussion, then the boys said, "What the fuck …" and Mike turned the music up again and they tried to outdo each other singing lyrics – so, once more, the car became a mini pub, full of cigarette smoke and beer breath and noise.

*

Outside, headlights fed on darkness. There was no right or left or up or down – just double yellow lines stretching away into the future.

*

When the car drifted momentarily, Mike said, "You okay, Skinny?"

"Of course, Mike. I'm right, right as rain."

Mike, being a man of action, had a solution. "Okay, boys, windows down, air-blast for Skinny."

The windows came down and icy air blasted through the car. Hamburger wrapping and serviettes flew about. Everyone laughed and swore. Then the windows came up again and the party resumed.

"Better now, Skinny?" Mike asked.

"Yeah, better, thanks," said Skinny, resuming his fidgeting. He swept his fingers through his hair over and over again. He pinched his arm till it hurt. He kept trying to focus on the dots of coloured light ahead that were moving about like fireflies. At least the smell of hops and fries and tobacco was gone.

*

Close to daybreak, everyone said they were busting, so Skinny found a bit of wide shoulder and pulled over and stopped the engine, and there was only the crunch of gravel and the sound of doors and nothing else.

They found themselves in a beautiful frozen world. Pastures sparkled in the starlight. Boulders dotted the shining fields like planets. The scattered, stunted trees were merely ragged absences of light. There were no cars or signs of human habitation. The motorway was far behind. Ahead of them, a long, straight, narrow road decanted itself into the moonless night.

They undid their zippers and directed golden arcs of steaming urine into the pools of darkness by the roadside.

*

When they got back in the car, it would not start.

The more Skinny tried, the more the starter motor faded – until there was nothing, not even the barest flicker of life from Mike's mother's beautiful machine.

"We're going to have to push it to get the engine turning over," said Solomon. "The road's pretty flat; might be even slightly down-hill from here."

So, they pushed while Skinny steered, everyone incorporeal on the night road. Shadow on shadow. Shade on shade – until a car passing the other way flashed it lights, confirming some residue of form.

Skinny leaned out the window to tell them that he was worried. "This is dangerous, guys. No-one can see us."

"Nah," said Mike. "She'll be right. We're picking up speed. Turn it over now, Skinny! Try now!"

Skinny turned the key again, but nothing happened.

Everyone said, "Fuck, fuck, fuck."

Then a set of equidistant lights appeared in the rear-view mirror. Big lights. Moving lights. Closing in.

"There's a truck coming, guys, a fucking truck!" Skinny shouted out the window.

"Don't worry, Skinny, don't be a fucking wuss," Mike replied. Mike was puffing. He could barely get the words out. Mike was never very fit.

The Volvo was gathering speed, and the boys were barely keeping up – but still the dashboard remained a brass rubbing of dead dials.

"What if it doesn't see us?"

"Sure it will. It'll overtake."

And then the stars went out, and the truck's high beam was illuminating everything – them, the valley ahead, the hills. Unrobed of darkness, the valley was waiting with insidious intent.

It was a paradox – this rate of change, these wicked shifting points of reference – fast, slow – all at once – pre-determined yet demanding self-determination. Would the truck make a wide pass? Would it not? Safer to assume the not. Wiser. Outside the car, in more leisured circumstances, he might have tossed a coin – but here he was, caught in the nanosecond, with a brain begging him to choose. And so he did. He chose. He veered hard to the left, careering the Volvo down a small slope while the boys screamed, "What the fuck!"

As he hit a tree, the truck passed by at speed on the same side of the road, trailing a single, long, Doppler-shifting rebuke, exactly as it should be: first lightning, then thunder.

Tossed from hill to hill, the horn blast lingered for some time – beyond the moment of impact, the hard reconciliation of carbon and metal, when Skinny lurched forward and whipped back, when the chassis crumpled and the bonnet lifted like a shucked oyster.

Skinny knew he was alive because he could hear Mike screaming at him. "You're a fucking loser, Skinny, I should never have invited you."

Skinny said nothing. Even after Solomon asked if he was okay and they tried to open the door, he just remained in his seat watching the little clouds of radiator steam rise up to join the Milky Way.

Finally, when a touch of colour appeared in the eastern sky, he climbed out through the back window to find the boys standing some metres behind the car, huddled in conference, apparently pondering their options.

Seeing Skinny, they made a tight huddle.

"We're just thinking," said Mike. "Give us a minute, will you?"

Skinny tried to interject. "There was nothing I could do, guys!"

"Fuck off, Skinny," Mike called out from the conclave.

So Skinny remained standing there, on the side of the road, contemplating himself, his friends, chaos theory and Nerida from Physics 2.

When he had thought enough, he retrieved his bag from the boot and began walking southwards with an arm out and a thumb up and the boys' eyes on his back.

It was a good season.

Before him, the snow-capped peaks were slowly gathering form.

OUT OF THE SKY

—

YOU COULD BARELY MAKE HIM OUT AT FIRST, A DISTANT FIGURE walking along a fence in a vast red landscape that was otherwise without boundary. A sentry line of posts stretched north and south. Close to the man the posts were well defined. Each carried the letters B H P in blisters of black solder. Through each post ran five taut wires, the uppermost barbed. But in the distance the posts lost form. They shimmered uncertainly and then seemed to float in the air before disappearing into the shifting light of summer heat.

Occasionally jet airliners arced high overhead. Thin white vapour trails lingered in a sky of perfect blue until currents of air gradually teased them into wisps of cloud. These passed unseen by the man, who remained absorbed in his task of inspection and repair. Except for the faintest humming of the wires, he could hear nothing. There was not the slightest breeze. Nothing challenged the stillness except his slow movement along the fence line. Now and then he would pause to work a piece of truant wire or kick away the wind-borne skeletons of plants with the stiff, economical action of an old man. Behind him trotted a dog, sniffing keenly for the scent of carrion. By two in the afternoon both man and dog were gone. A diminishing speck of white could be seen on the eastern horizon. A rolling plume of dust followed like the tail of a comet, splitting the visible world in two.

*

The windows of the ute were down, and the cabin was a maelstrom of wind and dust and the drum roll of heavy-tread tyres. It hadn't rained in months, and the sun had sculpted last season's puddles into endless ruts and corrugations. The dog struggled to keep its footing on the tray as the ute pitched and shuddered. The man was speeding. He had to be back in town by three. He would know his destiny at three.

After half an hour, dirt gave way to bitumen and the noise from the tyres abated. The man responded to this sudden peace by glancing to his left where compact discs lay strewn across the passenger seat. After a moment of consideration, however, he reached for a cigarette in his top pocket and lit up. Short square fingers fumbled with the dashboard lighter. He would have a smoke, but he was in no mood for music.

It was ten to three when he arrived at the clinic. The waiting room was crowded, as the doctors were running late. He took the last remaining seat, trying not to catch anyone's eye. He wondered whether he stank, as there had been no time for a shower.

Within moments a loud voice rang out: "Well, I'll be buggered, Bluey! Not you too, mate!"

And sure enough it was Boyd Carroll. He hadn't spoken to Boyd in years. He had tried to avoid him. Boyd, the school hero, the entrepreneur, the town worthy. His story was legendary: riches to rags to riches again with mining leases in booms and busts that came and went over the decades. Boyd had built a small empire while Bluey drifted from job to job. He was a plausible man.

Boyd was flanked by his second wife and their teenage son. Neither looked up. The wife kept to her magazine while the boy was bent over an iPhone.

"Can we swap places, love?" said Boyd to an old woman sitting on Bluey's right.

In moments he and Bluey were sharing reminiscences. They had worked together as station hands after leaving school. They had chased the same girls, drunk in the same pubs. It was Boyd who had found Bluey on the track after his motorcycle accident. Bluey had come off alone and was trying to crawl back to the main road with a broken leg. Boyd had saved his life. Boyd, the better man.

They were eventually interrupted by the receptionist who walked over to advise that "he won't be long".

At this juncture Boyd clapped Bluey on the shoulder and declared: "Well, Bluey, we've got to fight and we've got to win. The big C isn't going to get me: can't fit it into in the diary, mate."

"That's right, Dad, you'll beat it," piped up his son without lifting his eyes from his iPhone.

Boyd then returned to his family and Bluey returned to contemplating the patchwork quilt of fortune and misfortune which constituted his life. He sat bolt upright with hands on each thigh like a soldier awaiting court martial. Memories vaguely formed and dissipated as he stared at the three doors directly in front of him. Strange notions took hold. Bluey fancied that the first door represented reprieve; the third, hanging; and the middle door – well, that was the middle door. There was always a middle door: the door of real or false hope. It was like the pokies, he thought, plenty of chances but in the end the house wins.

It was no surprise to him, then, when the middle door opened and he was beckoned in by a doctor who seemed, predictably, much too young. He had flown in that morning from Sydney, bringing with him God's verdict. Out of the sky.

The doctor's words ran and coalesced like rivulets in a flood. Essentially, he offered Bluey chemotherapy and radiotherapy with a 50/50 chance of an extra year or two. When Bluey left the room (was it minutes? was it hours?) he gave Boyd no sign of triumph or defeat. He nodded in Boyd's direction and left the clinic, just as Boyd was also beckoned through Door 2.

Bluey drove home with a thick pile of notes on everything to do with his illness. He briefly considered reading them but then tossed the whole lot onto the kitchen table before going to his daughter's old room at the back of the house. He fancied that he felt her presence in the tiny particles of dust that rose and fell in the thin shafts of light from a window above her bed. She lived within the stale air. Her favourite dolls sat patiently on a shelf, and posters of rock idols clung precariously to the walls on balls of desiccating Blu Tack. Apart from these vestiges of family life, however, the room was crammed with mountains of opera recordings. Each LP, each CD, each cassette lay neatly stacked, ordered and catalogued. Bluey carefully selected an LP and took it to an old gramophone player in the living room. He turned the volume up and went and got a beer.

*

The following days went on much as usual. Bluey worked. He went to the club. He listened to music. Fortunately, he had a niece to help him with the arrangements.

"No, Robert (his real name) you can't have a smoking seat. Yes, Robert of course I'll look after Luciano (the dog). Yes, yes, I'll take Offenbach (the cockatiel) to my place. Come on Robert, look on the bright side, you haven't been to Sydney in years."

She was a sweet woman who had enough problems of her own, and he could not express anything but gratitude as she quickly condensed his life into a set of numbers: flights, hotels, appointments, admission dates, medical insurance, travel insurance and a raft of other details.

*

One of the most beautiful sunsets in living memory lit up the horizon on the day Bluey's niece drove him to the airport. The landscape was evaporating into dusky hues of green and blue as they reached the outskirts of town. A large ruby-red sun was receding into tufts of pink cumulus. The sky had an impossible translucency.

They pulled up outside the terminal entrance. His niece gave him a quick kiss with the engine running. She had to get home to feed the children, she said. There was no aircraft on the tarmac, but it would come. Boyd was also just getting out of a car. He had a bigger entourage with him this time. Bluey could hear the words of encouragement, the terms of endearment.

It was nearly two hours later when an aircraft finally accelerated along a line of fading white marks and took off into the night. Those on the ground marked its progress by sound alone, but for several minutes its navigation lights were clearly visible. They blinked sharply, urgently, in the black, moonless sky before being lost in an ocean of twinkling stars.

Just one person looked up to notice this union of temporal and eternal lights. He was sitting alone on a distant hill, facing the darkened plain. He was wearing a heavy coat, and a dog sat by his side. The "Addio del passato" from *La Traviata* filled the cold night air.

Bluey knew he was a happy man.

219

TELL US A BIT ABOUT YOURSELF

SHE SITS FACING A COMPUTER SCREEN AT THE BACK OF THE
house – in the room everyone calls the "office" because it is from
here that her mother runs the business of the family farm. She is
tense. Her back is ramrod straight, her forearms are resting on the
oak desk at neat right-angles and her eyes are fixed dead ahead like
the gaze of a dog who has just spotted a rabbit.

The room is bulging with boxes and books and files and the
sediment of generations: golf clubs, hockey sticks, photo albums,
game boards and twenty years' worth of *National Geographic*
magazines that cannot be thrown out because they belonged to
her mother's father. There is even a croquet set – a relic from the
golden years when lawns were green and mowed, when Pimm's
was drunk on Sunday afternoons.

The room would be claustrophobic were it not for a large
window looking out over the home paddock, the shearing sheds,
and, in the distance, a faint line of dark blue hills. It is mainly flat,
granite country – good soil when it rains; just dust in drought. The
periods where money is made are brief. There is wheat in the good
years and contracting work when things are desperate.

The farm carries three thousand sheep, give or take – depending
on dingos, boundary losses, thieving, natural attrition, and random

luck. Her father does the hands-on farming with just one full-time helper, George, who, truth be told, is past it. She had two brothers. Now she has one. Jim went off jackerooing, got into the booze, rolled his car near Wilcannia when he was only twenty-two. And there's Angus, working on an oil rig in the North Sea. Angus never gets in touch. Angus has a cold heart. Her mother has angina, so, it is up to her, Margot, the wonder girl, to take the overnight coach from Sydney when there's drenching or shearing on, or when her dad's back is playing up. It's a seven-hour trip. She does it every few months.

On the bare wall behind her are scattered small hooks and variations in paint tone suggesting the former presence of frames. Yesterday evening, her mother had taken down the family photographs, the award certificates, mainly prizes from when she was school dux, school captain, netball captain and just about everything else. Bella had advised her not to "give them any cues" – "them" being the people from the unfathomable world of the big organisation in the city she wants to join; "them" being the people who will interview her in a few minutes via Skype. Margot shuffles in her chair, rearranges the notes in front of her, takes a sip of water. *"They" had better not be late*, she thinks. *I'm psyched up. I cannot wait a moment longer.*

A sound of spurting steam is coming from the hallway. Her mother has probably moved the ironing board closer to be within earshot. Her mother shares her ambitions. "Never you mind about us," she said when the possibility of a prestigious city job came up. "You've got to make your own way – isn't that right, Jock?" It was after dinner several months earlier. Her father had his feet up in front of the TV. She knew she had to raise the subject before her father dozed off. He always dozed off around 8 pm with a half-drunk stubby of beer on the coffee table in front of him. He'd start work at the crack of dawn. It was understandable.

"Yeah," said her father. "She's got to do what's good for her." And for emphasis, "You're a good girl, Margot, you just do what you want to do and don't worry about us – we'll manage well enough." And that was it. Her father never wasted words. Her father was third generation on the farm and she, therefore, the fourth. The roots grow deeper.

She is well dressed to the level of her waist: white business blouse with a modest amount of make-up and hair done up in a bun – exactly the way Bella advised. Out of camera shot are dirty khaki shorts, a "lucky" plaited leather belt and thin long legs leading down to spotted socks. Her working boots are at the front door. It's the spring uni break; just one more term at university before graduation – an Arts/Law degree with honours, as everyone expected. *Margot delivers, Margot gets it done*, she thinks, *even if the price is bitten-down nails, sleepless nights and a history of anorexia*. She really wants this job. It involves helping people help themselves, which is her ideal.

The interview takes a few minutes to get underway because of poor reception. After some awkward verbal exchanges, a man and a woman materialise on the screen. They are about the age of her parents. The woman looks interested and possibly kind-hearted. The man seems bored. After brief eye contact and a "Good morning, Margot" he returns to looking down at something out of view.

The lady is in a business suit. She is wearing too much lipstick and her hair is surprisingly messy. There is a bookcase behind her laden with fat files in ring-binders. She tries to put Margot at ease with preliminary chit-chat about the airline strike and the drought. Then she says, "So, Margot, tell us a bit about yourself."

Margot glances at her crib cards. She knows she must incorporate the following words in her reply: —*diligent* —*passionate* —*curious* —*adaptable* —*resilient*. Bella said, "Trust me on this, Margot, darling." Margot manages to include all the words in her reply, but there is no time for self-congratulation because the next question follows hard upon the first.

Presumably, there are a lot of applicants. She wonders if the interviewers take it in turns to be "on the job." Clearly, it is the woman's turn.

The woman asks her about the "Indian Project." It is in her CV.

On the wall behind the screen, slightly to her right, is the word **INDIA** in bold black capitals on butcher's paper. There are bullet points below, a column of single words preceded by asterisks: —*stakeholders* —*respect* —*ethics* —*cultural sensitivity* —*change*. She expertly weaves them into a description of her university project about solar power in Indian slums. She does not mention the difficulties faced by a tall, blonde white woman with an interpreter trying to tie down slum-dwellers with a long questionnaire. She doesn't talk about the challenges of promoting solar panels to people living under leaking, corrugated iron roofs. "Keep everything positive", that's what Bella said. "You are lovely, the world is lovely; ergo, your words must be lovely." If Margot is one of the current young stars of country New South Wales, then Bella is exalted alumni. Bella is nearing the end of a highly contested graduate program herself. "You have to be holier than Jesus to get in," Bella advised.

Next comes a hypothetical scenario about a tricky situation, a wicked problem, as one of Margot's lecturers would call it. A crew member is very sick on a ship, having embarked with a slight fever. It is probably Ebola. There is a dilemma regarding isolation and the issue of compromising the ship's doctor and nurse. Margot wants to say that, being a country woman, she doesn't do hypotheticals; she just applies commonsense on a case-by-case, moment-by-moment basis; but she doesn't – she refers to a cue card headed: "Any hypothetical question", which is taped to a corner of her screen. The words —*refer* —*consult* —*protocol* —*team-oriented* roll smoothly off her tongue.

God, I'm a pro, she thinks.

Finally, the inevitable "working for us" questions arrive. This is on the butcher's sheet to Margot's left: —*self-motivated* —*account-able* —*committed* —*collaborative*. Margot pauses for a moment, thinking that no-one on Earth can get so many buzzwords into so few sentences. Then she draws a short breath, and a deluge of the right words roll naturally off her tongue – as fluently as her very good French.

"Thank you," the interviewers say. "We will be in touch late October." The man was apparently paying attention at the end – surely a good sign.

The screen goes blank. Margot stands up and stretches and asks the spider near the window, "Well, Mr Daddy Long-Legs, how did I go?"

Every muscle in her body begins to ease. She gets up and leaves the room to talk to her mother in the hallway. She sees that only one pillowslip has been ironed.

"How'd it go, love?" her mother asks, putting the iron down and searching her face for clues.

"Pretty good, I think, not bad, about what I expected."

Margot goes to the kitchen and gets a beer and returns to continue talking to her mother, but her mother cuts her short. "Dad's just been on the radio. He's wondering whether you can take the quad bike out to Wattle Creek with half-a-dozen star posts and the post driver. Also, wire from the back shed. Sorry, love – tree's fallen across the fence and George is in town. I've got a nice roast going for you when you get back."

*

The spot is twenty minutes' ride away, and her father already has a large casuarina in pieces by the time she arrives. Great slices of dismembered tree lie scattered around a ragged hole in the fence. A cooling chainsaw rests on the back of the ute. Her father, now in his late fifties, a little paunchy in the belly, is sitting on one of the logs, having a rest. His shirt is soaked in sweat, the front of which is dirty white, the back almost grey with flies. A few remaining strands of his once fine, dark head of hair are plastered across his forehead, mixed with sawdust and dirt. Margot marvels that he has done it all by himself. She worries for her dad. She imagines him dying alone one day – out in the middle of nowhere. A heart attack, an accident – it happens.

"Lightning strike," he says as she approaches. He seldom indulges in the luxury of verbs. She knows he means that the tree was weakened a while ago by lightning and now, finally, it has given up the ghost. She can see the tell-tale bits of charcoal amongst its ruins.

Then her father says, "Thanks, Margot. Great girl!" and they unload the posts and the very heavy coil of smooth wire. The barbed wire has recoiled on either side of the hole like two halves of a cut snake. She knows he'll reuse the barbed wire. In all things, he is economical.

*

On the way home, she thinks about her life back in Sydney, about her boyfriend – or, probably, soon to be ex-boyfriend. James is smart, ambitious, muscled from early morning gym sessions – but he's not a real man, she thinks, not like her dad or her brother. James is a verbal warrior. He thrusts and parries with nouns and verbs – in a good way – to good purpose – it's understandable – what else is there in a city other than words? Being good at words herself, she knows that there is opportunity in the city. Somewhere, buried in the concrete and glass, there must be a treasure trove of success and fulfilment. That's the logic – but she finds the pull of open landscape hard to resist, the gravity of empty space. There is something compelling about a life lived largely without dialogue, a life unedited by intellectuals. It's in her blood, after all. And what is James? All talk, all city. If she's going to live in the city, she at least needs a man who has a bit of country in him, a bit of sky in his eyes. She remembers a recent foreshore walk in Sydney. She and James had only just begun when the weather changed and a thin curtain of light rain began falling across the scene before them – the purple bay, the sleepy federation houses, the pale eucalypts, the tidy, bobbing boats. Just as she was thinking how lovely it all was, James piped up and said: "Let's go back, it's getting wet." And then then there was the fuss of dealing with muddy shoes in his new Audi.

When she is roughly halfway along the shortcut to the homestead, she finds a roo caught in the fence line, its hind-leg snared between two strands of overlapping wire, suspended at a terrible angle. The strangeness of this is unsettling – the most sure-footed of creatures upside down – immobilised. She can tell by the matted fur, the arc of flattened dirt and grass, that the animal has been lying there for at least a day or two.

She dismounts and approaches the poor creature. The leg is broken, yet the animal is very quiet. Everything, in fact, is very quiet. In the back blocks, late in the day, when the sun is setting behind the hills and there's no wind, the silence is almost absolute. The silence of country distressed the early settlers. The First Peoples dealt with it. They talked. They sang. They moved about in songlines.

The roo is looking at her, not in terror, but with resignation. She can see the flecks of brown and blue in its eyes – and, also, the reflection of passing clouds. It is breathing quick, soft, shallow breaths.

She goes back to the quad and gets a skinning knife and stands by the roo, with the silver blade catching the last of the sunlight. With her left hand, she draws its head gently backwards and with a single, swift stroke she cuts its throat and steps back, knife at her side, watching the creature's eyes grow dull, the ground darken around its neck.

She drags the roo clear of the fence and, realising that it is a female, checks the pouch. To her relief there is no joey. Several hundred metres away, before a copse of she-oak, a big buck roo is watching. She knows the rest of the mob are also there, out of sight, waiting for nightfall, when they will return to sniff about and accept what is, what must be.

Walking back to the quad, she says softly: "You want me to tell you a bit about myself? Well, this is a bit about myself."

ACKNOWLEDGEMENTS

I would like to thank the following people for their help in developing these stories from their first tiny iterations to their final fruition, often after many revisions:

My anthology editor, Jane Smith, for her great insights, literary skill and patience with my IT incompetency.

Ann Dettori of Independent Ink for helping me realise this project with sure-footed expertise.

Daniela Catucci of Catucci Design for her superb cover design.

My wife Philippa Shelley Jones for her patience and editorial skills and my children, Hannah, Charlie and Phoebe, for their love and encouragement.

Other professional editors have also helped enormously with some of the stories in this collection: Nick Atanasoff, David Brookes, Trevor Byrne (Hyland & Byrne) and Kate Steele.

Finally, I am grateful to a number of friends who have made helpful contributions over the years as early readers: Ayse Mikkelsen, Nerida Hackenberg, Michelle Dunn, Graham Lowry-Jones, Mark and Tiffany Donnelly, Julia Lee, Laurel Hixon, Brian Dalton and David Ward.

ABOUT THE AUTHOR

My first publications were related to obstetrics and gynaecological surgery, exciting in their own way, but not as exciting as an all-night drive to the snowfields with a car full of drunken undergraduates, or buying masterpieces from a great artist in her infirmity, or abandoning Ted Leary to his fate in the outback – fictional ideas arising from what I have self-diagnosed as an over-active, possibly aberrant, imagination.

I decided early on that if I had no success with my stories, I would abandon the project; fortunately, a string of literary competition wins and shortlistings have kept me at it. I should probably work in my off-grid caravan in the high country of southern New South Wales – only, I don't; I find the bush just too engaging, with its hidden worlds, its silences and sometimes ringing voice, so I write in the city, listening to cars and people and an irregular menagerie of creatures: kookaburras, roof possums, parrots and, if the wind is in the right direction, the roar of lions from the nearby zoo.

Living in these circumstances, with a lovely wife and family, a sheepadoodle and a farm shed stocked with emergency supplies, I count myself a lucky man.

A novel is in progress.

www.ingramcontent.com/pod-product-compliance
Lightning Source LLC
Chambersburg PA
CBHW050616190726
48283CB00007B/2436